Distant Voices

An anthology of stories from the University of Hull Creative Writing MA Online

Autumn 2021 Cohort

Various Authors

Dedication

To the lecturers, tutors and supervisors who have taught us.

And to the Covid Cohort who have worked, worried and wept together over the past two years, and learned how to carry each other all the way over the finish line.

CHRISTOPHER WESTOBY

Some of us embark upon a Creative Writing MA because there is a specific piece of work we already have in mind, or perhaps have already begun, and we are seeking to develop our skillset in order to make this project the best it can be. Some of us aren't too sure what we're destined to write but we know an MA will give us the strongest footing and even catalyse a dormant idea. Some of us, myself included, begin an MA as one type of writer and graduate as something else entirely. It can be a rough ride.

Programme Founder Martin Goodman was a tutor of mine when I took an MA Creative Writing many years back. He warned me not to do anything drastic with my life whilst doing this course: don't break up with your partner or move to a new country. Writing this intensely can really destabilise the ground beneath you. You're being pushed into territories that are new, uncomfortable. You're submitting your writing to be critiqued every week. You don't always get the grade you anticipated, sometimes for what feels like your best work yet. You're always making sense of your own thoughts, imagination, and how this translates to the future reader. But in this whirlwind emerges excellent writing and excellent writers.

The authors in this collection are just that. They bravely undertook an MA in an online format new to our university. The many virtues of this include finding like-minded writers in any corner of the world. Their writing throughout the past two years has undergone a remarkable development and I am thrilled to see it showcased now.

Martin Goodman

The writers in this book are all pioneers. They took a leap of faith and became the first cohort in the new online Masters in Creative Writing from the University of Hull.

What did that mean? That writing was of primal importance to them. And it was no longer good enough to write as well as you can. You could do better than that.

The pieces here have all been meticulously shaped and redrafted, because that's what writers do. They guide the reader steadily into a realm of wild imagination. However controlled the tale, it's built from the merest puff of an idea. Characters, place, sights, sounds, smells, plot, all accrue out of a writer's first sense that yes, here perhaps is a story worth the telling.

These writers come from around the world, with such a range of life experiences that you would not expect to find them in the same room. Yet for years they have shared an intense life together. They have dared to try out new ways of writing, and open themselves to feedback. Does it connect? Why? Why not? Sometimes they were thrilled by what other writers said, and sometimes they were hurt. And they kept trying harder, coming back for more, because that's how good writing is made.

Two years on, that Masters course complete, the qualifications are collected, and here's where all that work and dedication takes fire.

In you, the reader.

Welcome to this very fine collection.

Your mind is where these stories can finally ignite.

Contents

VERONIQUE GUIBERTEAU CANFRERE

Dare I tell you fantasy? I may claim that at ten years old I wrote my first novel. The bare truth is that I hated writing before 2012.

Nevertheless, in my playpen I started my reader journey, manically deciphering backwards a drug dictionary my father had discarded inside the enclosure. I've never stopped since. I loved Flaubert at nine, I hated Hugo at ten, and waited till seventeen to spend a summer In Search of the Lost Time. In my teens, I boarded a spaceship for dystopian galaxies I still revisit from time to time.

When I embedded with the medical studies, Joyce Carol Oates was a permanent fixture on my reading log. Since 2000, I have resumed a steadier reading pace, exploring the worlds of Jane Austen, Henry James, and Raymond Carver, to name but a few.

As many, school initiated my writing endeavours with "what I did on holidays" assignments, then came the formal essays about literature and philosophy to complete my secondary education. The painful pathway went on with clinical articles about debilitating conditions. After I quit surgery, I foolishly expected a reprieve: I spent nights on commercial proposals. But in 2012, a bonus target—

writing blog posts for the corporate website—ignited the writing spark.

Since then, I have devoted the energy that made me a surgeon and a global company manager to learning the craft: reading, writing stories, and studying for a Master of Arts at the University of Hull (2019-2021).

I have never published fiction.

NOUNOURS

I'm a Catholic teddy bear. I've heard more Hail Marys than I'd have liked. Even now, Ms Grody drones on. Listen!

"Hail Mary full of Grace the Lord is with thee. Who's this lord? ... Blessed art thou among women. Wasn't blessed myself. Teddybear! Don't look at me like that."

Bear in mind, my name is not Teddybear. My first name is Nounours, but for a long time nobody's called me Nounours.

"Hail Mary mais ou et ... zeit von zu."[1] Can't she stop that litany? God be praised! Ms Grody no longer reads aloud *The Imitation of Christ*[2]: she's blind. The book lies beside me on the windowsill. Last year, when we moved into the Our Lady's Nursing Home, I tried being sociable; to no avail. I'm on my own, facing Ms Grody's monstrous armchair: no fancy upholstery, just a sensible maroon faux leather. The book can't speak, but on its cover, above a bearded man looking more thoughtful than joyful, the title and a quote are written in gold letters. You wonder why I'm so well-read: lucky fluke in an ocean of misfortune where Ms Grody's taken the first place since Elsie and I met her fifty years ago.

---

[1] French and German textbooks collected dust on her shelves. Ms Grody fancied herself being well versed in foreign languages. She has never been.

[2] Ms. Grody and her devout cronies luxuriated in this book. Thomas a Kempis (c.1380-1471) is very pleased in heaven.

Elsie was a nice and whiny four-year-old. So nice that Santa brought her a special gift on Christmas Day: me, soon after christened Nounours.[3] In May, Elsie was sent to kindergarten. There, a tall lady ushered us to the cloakroom.

"Hello, I'm Ms Grody."

Ms Grody was prettier than Elsie's Mummy, but her smile hid her teeth.

"Leave your teddy bear here," she said to a wailing Elsie. At the end of the day, Elsie ran through the gate, holding out a doodle.

"Look Mummy! Our house and Dad and you and me and Tobbydog!" She forgot all about me. After a week I spent on a shelf, Ms Grody took me home and threw me in the upper drawer of her dresser where I would sit among flyers, notices, and dirt, until last year.

Ms Grody taught English at her home. I listened to the lessons she drilled into five-year-olds.

"This is ..." or "Show me ..." A few months later, I could've whispered the answers through the keyhole. I could've boasted of my prowess: I could read 'Take a girl like Lulu' on the flyer beside me. I was lucky; Ms Grody often discarded flyers in the drawer and if they landed the right way up, I'd get more food for my studious mind. I read 'Naughty but Nice,' 'Catch the Wave. Coke,' or 'Enlightenment from Cadbury.'

"Let Jesus be in you! Be pure and free within, unentangled with any creature!" When Ms Grody screams, it's because she's hungry.

---

[3] Elsie's French grandmother chose the name and didn't yield when a stream of tears drenched me.

To be honest, when two smooth globes stretched her blouse, Ms Grody was often entangled, mostly with the man in black. Sometimes he came when the children were there; she called him Father. Sometimes he came when she was alone; she called him Fuckmedeep and held her skirt high above her thighs. And after he left, Ms Grody would get into a frenzy: rushing to the garden, running back, lifting her dishevelled blouse to encase her waist in a barbed wire belt.

"Suffer with Christ ..." she yelled, bowed over the book laid open on the table,

"... and for Christ if you wish to reign with Him." She kissed the book before resuming her frantic pacing around the room.

"Please Lord, and give me the strength to suffer for You." As far as I know, the Lord never answered. Soon, she would give up, snatch the thorns from her skin, and mutter for hours.

She spoke only English then, not gibberish.

"Mais ou et donc or ni car aus bei mit nach zeit von zu."

"Ms Grody, stop that silliness! Lunch time!" the nurse shouts.

"Shut up, Teddybear! Maisouetdonc ... The Kingdom of God is within you!"

"Ms Grody, get up or I'll hide your beloved Teddybear."

I don't think I'm so beloved, but for sure I'm fed up with 'Teddybear'. Nobody bothers to give me a name. I want a proper one.

Maisouet? It ends like a croaky voice.

Nachzeitvon? A mouthful of a name, isn't it?

Ornicar? Yeesss! That's a good one.[4]

Ornicar the proud teddy bear who (I'm not something, I'm someone) long ago was Nounours.

Nounours Ornicar. Sounds great, doesn't it?[5]

---

[4] The English version, however neither because, is as a mouthful as nacht zei von, not suitable for a proper and elegant name. I can't imagine being called Nounours Howeverneitherbecause. I chose the French one: or ni car.

[5] Bless you, writers who "show me the path I should walk" (Psalms 143:9).

PERSUADERS

I've always loved the title sequence of The Persuaders! You know, this 70s series where two men from different backgrounds chased criminals together.

Today I Tidy My Desk.

The day after tomorrow, I go on a pastoral trip to a Pacific island to support official peace talks. Meanwhile, my study and my bedroom will be renovated and insulated: the icy air of the Roman winter seeps through the windows of our grandiose Renaissance palaces. Good riddance to the gildings! Out the golden cherubs laughing on the top of the huge mirror beside my bed! For too long, these angelic creatures have silently made fun of my sagging flesh. They don't suit the required austerity of an organisation that preaches the virtues of poverty. Sometimes, my predecessors forgot the core principles.

This refurbishment is an opportunity to sort and remove my personal papers from prying eyes; especially these diaries from my debut 25 years ago. To be appointed deputy undersecretary of a cardinal just after graduating had been an honor and a let-down. My fellows begrudged my position in the Curia; even a lowly one is an object of desire. His Eminence was mostly interested in intrigue and young priests–I can't deny I was one of them–, and my grandmother died that year. I took up writing to unwind and to ponder the gap between my naïve ideal of sanctity and my solitary existence in the crowded snake pit I lived in. Weird to revisit who I was. I can't feel anymore the turmoil. Helping people gives meaning and worthiness to the vow of celibacy I took long ago.

Last week, I read in McKinsey Facts–their consultants re-engineered the Vatican communication departments–that the biggest challenge CEOs face is isolation. I am not the CEO of the Catholic Church, I'm just one of its Chief Officers. McKinsey suggests 'recovery practices': spirituality, reading, exercise, and family or friends. Easy for the first three: spirituality is part of my job, I've always been an avid reader, and at 51 I'm young enough to take up running. Trickier for the family and friends' practices: companionship has been rarifying since I left the Pontificia Università Gregoriana; my siblings built their lives far away; and obviously by trade, I don't have a spouse. I can't imagine the Catholic Church repealing its own version of 'Don't ask Don't tell' in the foreseeable future.

Pacific Paradise

"Ouch! Fuck this hike!" someone shouts behind me.

"Don't be such a pussy Garcia! It's just a pebble. And put a shirt on! We're not only with our usual bunch of journalists," another voice mutters.

"Fuck you, Steve! I do as I want; this guy is not going to stop me."

Me, 'this guy', and a group of reporters are tramping across a primary forest to meet in 'private' with Chief Nouak. The talks with the Prime Minister's envoy haven't worked so well. It is time for me to step onto the stage. My esteemed colleagues are too old for this field trip. When we left, the rabbi and the imam were comfortably ensconced in the lounge chairs by the swimming pool, a pot of tea between them, arguing over tricky tiny points of theology.

Me, 'this guy', is quite pleased to stroll through the heart of this island, and for once to ditch the Roman collar and the black wool suit. Nevertheless, khaki shorts and tee shirt don't do the trick: my little company can't forget with whom they are trekking.

"Garcia, he's nice, not so stiff and in good shape for a prelate. Most of them spend their time talking around tables laden with gourmet food under the gold trimmings of their holy palaces," the guy named Steve said.

"He has a nice ass; I'll give you that."

I don't turn my head. It gets warmer under the canopy, but it's refreshing to be a nice ass past fifty and in my position. The seminarists, as enticing as they are, dare not utter a word about my behind, even in the throes of passion. I love this phrase, but I'm not sure the young and ambitious who surround me wherever I go in Rome surrender to these throes. I don't mind. I was like them.

"I can't appreciate it as you do, Garcia."

"Steve, don't worry, I would never comment on yours." Garcia laughs. "And yes, I appreciate it a lot and I wouldn't refuse to shag him if he asked."

I focus on stepping over fallen mossy branches, the last barrier before an unexpected clearing scattered with boulders.

"We can stop there to drink and snack." The guide spreads his hands, pointing to the makeshift seats. Garcia and Steve settle on the farthest rock from me. Steve halves a mango. Garcia sucks the fruit, the juice rolling down his naked torso.

Nice pecs.

He looks up and we stare. He blushes, it's weird on a tanned skin. He stands up and crosses the clearing. Towering over me, he sweeps back a black strand, inhales, and stutters,

"Your ... Excellence ... Please ... Excuse me!"

"For what?"

"For the cursing!"

I smirk. "And for the nice ... ?"

His cheeks redden. He mumbles. "It wasn't about you."

"I'm disappointed." I look up straight into his blue eyes.

Garcia smiles.

The Catholic News Agency tweeted last month, 'New curial constitution to be released: Pope can count on the youngest cardinal of the Curia he created last year to rejuvenate Catholicism.'

And the newly appointed journalists start touring the Curia today, visiting twenty of us in two days. Great! If I do the math, not more than a fifteen-minute meeting, no time for idle chat. The mandatory photo call takes seven minutes: as usual I'll display my best profile framed by the brocade curtain on a background of terracotta Vatican roofs. Plus three minutes to say hello and two minutes for goodbye before they are ushered into the parlor to have a coffee or whatever stale drink the nuns would fancy to offer. It leaves three minutes for conversation. I assume I may talk about the frescoes. I give a fresco speech every week to Polish miners or Columbian policemen. A safe topic.

Let's look at the brief the Osservatore Romano sent.

Drew Adwart The Guardian,

Kurt Vornschuller Die Zeit,

Jacques Tancrede Le Monde,

Eduardo Garcia El Pais.

The Garcia of the island?

I peer at the thumb nail beside the names: longish black hair and light eyes. It's the one who ate mangos, bare chested, three years ago in the primary forest. I shouldn't revisit those feelings… dumbass hypocrite Jesuit… you dreamt of the mango juice.

The baroque clock chimes, its cherubs hammering the motionless golden goats pulling their chariot. A knock, a black robe walks in, bows, and hushes, "Your Eminence, the journalists would be honored to meet you."

Following the usual ceremonial, I stand up, bypass the desk, but don't go further than one meter beyond it. The middle of the room is for lowly clergymen, the two-third for the ambassadors to the Holy Seat, and close to the door for my fellow prelates. One by one they eminence me.

Garcia's smile highlights his tanned skin, and spreads to mischievous eyes.

"Your Eminence, congratulations and I'm pleased to see you again."

After the group photo, I direct them to the settee and chairs, stiff enough to prevent any lounging. Visitors aren't to get cosy here.

"Are you well accommodated? Navona hotel?"

They mumble, "Vespasiano."

"Rome is the city of art. Did you notice the frescoes in the staircase?"

They nod.

"Michelangelo's first assistant led this fine rendition of the epic battle between Good and Evil with angels fighting demons for the True Faith. You're welcome to visit again to study the details, the embossed armors, the blood seeping through the fabrics, or the pain-contorted faces."

The Guardian fiddles with her purse handle. Die Zeit and Le Monde examine their nails. On time, a black robe opens the parlor door and utters, "Would you like a drink?"

Garcia lingers, "Your frescoes: gore and hardcore sex artfully packaged in a Holy War."

"Aren't you a Catholic Mr Garcia?"

"Yes, I was."

"And now?"

"Nothing. It faded long ago. Too hypocritical for my taste."

A painful echo to my doubts.

He bows, "I am coming again soon to scrutinize those young male bodies."

Garcia's Diary -12-

Indeed, I came back, many times.

First for the fresco that eventually revealed an undercover Saint Sebastian: one of the fighters, stripped naked, his 'vital' parts fortunately removed from prudish eyes by a pennant. Nothing said then but allusions to the gay culture amid reminiscences of the primary forest. A

20

week after, under the guise of an interview (still to be written), we talked and drank freshly grounded coffee. More espressos or teas or wanderings to admire again and again the fresco (cardio step workouts of sorts) developed into a weekly (daily?) kind of pilgrimage to his Renaissance palace; a break from the hustle bustle; discussions, jokes, and smiles I didn't know I needed.

But this morning I barged in his study and slammed my smart phone on his desk.

"Look! How can you support this?"

He read the tweet 'US Conference of Catholic Bishops: fighting abortion is a preeminent goal over poverty or justice.' He sighed and when he took off his reading glasses, I could see the weariness clouding his eyes.

"You don't have to abide by the rules and the dogma of the Catholic Church you left long ago."

"I know! But you, how can you agree with this!"

"I don't."

Garcia's Diary -17-

Running is a great way to forget. A shrink would invoke sublimation, a biochemist endorphin, or a priest mystic experience.

Today, I sweated for five kilometers on the dusty tracks of Casa de Campo. Fantasies of making out with the cardinal I missed too much for my sanity, are gone with the liquid pouring from my pores. Nice way to say, fuck off! I don't want to daydream about you! The Monsignor into Spanish gutters!

Easy task in Madrid far from the 'enticing pleasure of conversation' with the said cardinal. To cool down, on the way back to my car parked close to Palacio Real, I walked through the Campo del Moro and took a detour to avoid Catedral de Santa Maria. I didn't want to light a votive candle. I didn't want to pray. I haven't for so long.

Garcia's Diary -21-

He wanted to go somewhere with me.

Pointing to the sepia vignettes scattered on an ancient map of Rome behind his desk, he asked me if I had already visited this church or that basilica. He asked mostly about ecclesiastic places. Not surprising given his trade.

"Garcia, we could visit the catacombs of San Sebastiano."

I wasn't so eager to see catacombs. Wandering through graveyards is not what I call a pleasant outing. But cardinals are not supposed to go out on a date.

In the fumes of Rome's traffic, I waited for him at Metro Colosseo, not far from the Vatican but not too close: people could recognise him. He craves being incognito. Bus 118 shook us on Via Appia Antica, the road of our musty Latin textbooks. I braced myself against the aisle armrest to avoid bumping into him.

"You ditched the red attire," I said.

"Most occasions don't require full regalia."

"Bad for me, I love the cappa magna."

"We don't wear so often the cappa magna. Since 1969's reforms. Update your references, dear Garcia." The 'dear' took me aback. His eyes stayed riveted on the antique cobblestones.

We got off the bus beside a concrete yard leading to a modest white portico with three mannerist arches. I had pictured basilica San Sebastiano fuori le mura as a grandiose cathedral, the proper seat for the cardinal-priest he told me he was to justify this choice of excursion. It was sunny and mild, the stone pines aromatic fragrance purifying the polluted air. A dark opening loomed in the middle of the colonnade. We were going to visit the dead.

Formaldehyde, the acrid smell surrounding my father when every week I went to his floor, the Anatomy floor of the School of Medicine. He would say, "Wait here." I've never entered the rooms. From time to time a student rushed out, and I glimpsed rows of polished wheeled tables where grey flesh was exposed, surrounded by pimpled young grown-ups laughing to repel sick and choke. Death will always be this mephitic stench oozing from the Anatomy department.

A wrinkled Brother lost in the pleats of his rough cowl greeted us and grasped our coins without looking up.

"Sirs, this way."

A bony hand emerged from the brown sleeves to point at a marbled plate engraved with Latin letters above the stairs plunging to the catacombs.

"This was gifted by our beloved cardinal who blessed the new altar a year ago. One of his rare visits."

The beloved cardinal in black chinos and blue T-shirt benevolently smiled and grabbed my biceps. "Thank you. Come."

I could smell the acrid death. We went down graveled stairs. Elbows bumped rough stone walls. The end of the tunnel would unveil a room adorned with stacks of skulls and clothed skeletons. I had seen that on the website Catacomb.it. These bones had been somebody long ago. They weren't anymore.

"Lower your head. People then were shorter than you are."

We followed narrow corridors dotted by hollowed niches the size of a small human body. He babbled. I heard nothing. The pungent smell of my youth engulfed me in white sound, an airtight bubble.

"Look!" We stepped into a creamy room; a delicate framework of ochre lines enclosed Roman frescoed figures, animals, and flowers. The bubble popped. Only mould and dust. No skull. I exhaled.

"Garcia, you are pale. Are you claustrophobic?"

"No. I don't like death."

Garcia's Diary -35-

I reread the previous entries: they don't make sense. Usually writing helps me think about what happens in my life. I need it now.

Outings became real dates, escapes from the baroque jail, where high walls enclose narrow passageways swarming with black robes that shift into furtive shapes after sunset. I had to 'leash' him to avoid the vultures. A rather handsome, not so old and not so paunchy cardinal could attract them like honey. As a journalist, I know it by trade: paparazzi can embellish mundane activities with juicy bits to attract readers, 'An affair in the Curia: the Robert De Niro cardinal got a boyfriend.' After the first months, he wanted more and me too. Past the dull behaviour of a seasoned prelate, he is funny, caring and smart. He hates the hypocrisy prevailing within the Church. More a sex expert than you would imagine a prelate to be and theoretically a marriage scholar by trade, he didn't have a clue on how a relationship works: sharing inner thoughts, being tender, or opening up to another soul were foreign territories. He was an innocent.

One night, after another round of herbal tea, we faced each other on the stiff settee, our hands close enough to feel a tentative brush from time to time.

"Inside your Eternal City, you've got a twisted vision of relationships. Young men for hidden sex and pompous talks with your fellows. You're alone."

"No!"

"At midnight you're alone. You may have fulfilled your sex cravings, your brain cravings, and maybe your friendship cravings, but at the end you're alone."

"I have my family."

"Really? Don't they host you more than welcome you?"

He looked to our hands.

"Yes, you're right. The priesthood put a distance between me and them; except my mother but now she's gone. I'm no longer somebody's child."

"Me neither."

He glanced up and cradled my hands.

"We are two lonely bearded babies wailing in concert."

I took the helm. Besides shagging here or there, I've always loved romancing even though I haven't practiced a lot. On a weekend in Aosta Valley in a rented cabin, safe from prying eyes, we eventually acted on our attraction.

And I'm more hooked than before. What's the next step? I thought that we could enjoy a light thing tightly framed by our jobs' demands. I don't feel it now. It's going out of control. I'm lost. And him? He can't display his special someone in full light.

Time to get out of this, to store it in memories I will revisit in my old age. Better for him. Far better.

Garcia's Diary -36-

In Galleria Alberto Sordi, I bought a tee-shirt (with two penguins on the ice cap) now packed beside the letter in brown paper with the mention: Riservato - all'attenzione da sua Eminenza il cardinale…

I asked to be relocated. In a week, I am moving to Helsinki. The cold will be a nice change, won't it?

Yesterday, I Received a Parcel.

As usual, I get up at 6:30 a.m. I kneel, a praying habit ingrained by my grandmother when I was five. Then I praised God for the day I had enjoyed, and I prayed Him for helping me grow into a righteous altar boy. For a decade, I haven't been so eager to speak to the Lord, but I have never given up the sacred time, a tribute to Granny. She died the year I was ordained. A frail, hunched, white shape had been wheeled through the cathedral. She wanted to see me prostrating in front of the altar. She passed away a fortnight after. I blessed her body and led the service. I can't remember grieving: the rites and the promise of the afterlife helped me cope. The hope of seeing her again faded and then vanished. Now, I know she is gone forever. What would she have said about my decision?

Joints creaking, I stand up. I need to work out more. After today, I will go running with Garcia.

Shower, shampoo, grey hairs swirling through the drain. At this rate they'll soon all be gone.

A knock at the door. The bass voice of my deputy secretary. "Your Eminence, would you like me to help you dress?"

"No, thank you Father Andrea." Before, I used to grasp these opportunities to unwind before the busy day.

The golden candelabras loom upon my private altar. In my years in Nigeria, I celebrated Mass every morning for a crowd sharing with me the joy of the liturgy. I no longer see the point of reciting the Missal by rote.

A knock at the door. The housekeeper's soft voice. "Your Eminence, breakfast is served." People whisper that Sister Elsa is in love with me. I hope she has a special friend among her battalion of young novices dusting, cooking, doing the laundry for us, Princes of the Church. I don't want to be one of them anymore, only his Prince Charming forever. A cheesy thought.

"Good Morning, my dear brothers." I smile. Twenty black-clad men stand up around the white table bedecked with the ancient silverware the nuns have polished with religious zeal for ages.

A cup of coffee and a spoonful of scrambled eggs later, I retreat to my study.

"Your Eminence, the minutes of the building site meeting." After the appalling fire that five years ago triggered a flare of sorrow, faith and money, Notre Dame reconstruction had been the overarching project of my tenure, from afar admittedly. A genuine, committed and faithful cardinal will consecrate the new cathedral. Not I. No need to read the report from my secretary. Better go to the library.

In the hallway, I come across an army of young men, flaring cassocks fitting chiselled torsos. Two years ago, I would have smiled, talked, and sent a subdued invitation to my library to the most appealing, to stroke the worn-out leather, pet the golden letters, and cuddle the dotted soft paper. A knowing look, and we would have gone to the rear door of my bedroom. They weren't repelled by my old body, even though I wasn't a fool misled by the mischievous smiles and the bold touches. I have also been young and ambitious, longing to flatter the powerful and to purge the sexual drive of my twenties. Since Garcia, I no longer crave these stealth encounters that fuelled my life, first as a puppy eager to please, and then as the instigator willing to seduce.

In the darkest nook of the library, on a gilded lectern under a glass cover, sits the illustrated Bible. Once again, I marvel at the intricate pictures Middle Age monks drew hunched day after day above their table surrounded by inkstands drooling a rainbow. Before Garcia, while meditating in front of the illuminations, a hot wave swelled my heart, the remnant of my childhood love for God, the one that pulled me into clerical life, the only way to fill the hole I felt when I wasn't praying on the marbled church floor. It was a mere infatuation. I still believe in something. I don't love it anymore. I've got somebody who speeds my pulse.

Until sunset, I browse through the books, making mental snapshots of the room where I have spent so many soothing hours. I will miss the library. Having dinner alone is a dull affair. I swallow a cup of bisque, bite in a chunk of cheese, gulp a glass of red wine, nod to the nuns' shadowy shapes and head to my bedroom. I pat the shepherd, the dove, and the flock of sheep frolicking on the cross jutting forward, propelled by my comfortable–as Garcia says–stomach, and eventually take off the pectoral cross: I won't ever feel its weight again.

I reread my resignation e-mail and hit 'Send'. The formal letter is already in the out-basket.

I put on the tee-shirt with the two penguins. Tonight, I don't need a book to help sleep come, to forget what I don't have. I will have it tomorrow, forever.

TIM BARLOW

Tim Barlow has long been fascinated by sailing and the sea, as you can tell from Atlantic Crossing, his contribution to this anthology. The piece is an extract from a longer work which is under construction. Tim is a law librarian by profession, and has also been a tax inspector, an engineer, an MP's research assistant and a publican. His first degree was in Politics and Government. He was born and bred in Derbyshire, far from the sea in the middle of England, but he migrated south to London and now lives with his wife Paula and son Rafferty in Hastings, on the south coast, within sight of the English Channel. Tim's only previous published works have been reviews of music gigs in for local newspapers. He has been scribbling away and trying to get published since he and a friend, Ralph, created a short adventure book – Mansion of No Return - during their lunch breaks at primary school in 1970. The sole copy survives and the film rights are available for purchase. To see more of Tim's work, head to https://writertim.blogspot.com/

ATLANTIC CROSSING

One September evening Tom Hobbs arrived at Hull marina carrying all his possessions in a holdall. He walked to the Minerva pub, but paused outside, cutting a tall, slim figure against the dusk. That morning he had clipped his dark hair short and shaved off his usual stubble; a new look for a new life. He savoured the view. To the west the sun dripped gold above the suspension bridge, and across the Humber to the south the lights on the flatlands and ferry terminals of Lincolnshire glimmered in the last rays of daylight.

After a few minutes a stranger joined him at the quayside, nodded towards Tom's holdall and said, 'You here to meet Skipper Bob?'

'Yep.'

'Me too. I'm Ralph.'

Tom guessed that Ralph was in his thirties, like himself, but Ralph's weathered complexion and goatee beard made him look older. A shaggy mane of straw-coloured hair cascaded down to the collar of his rugby shirt. He was a few inches shorter than Tom, and a few inches broader. They shook hands. Ralph's palm was hard, Tom noticed, the skin of a regular sailor.

'I'm Tom. Good to meet you. Do you know what Bob looks like?'

'Nope. Shall we go inside?'

'Sure.'

They settled at a large wooden table in the triangular bow of the pub and watched the great brown river ebbing silently eastwards into the North Sea. Ralph sipped his beer, offered Tom a cigarette and asked him where he was from.

'Nottingham.' It was a lie. 'You?'

'Down south, originally,' Ralph answered, vaguely. 'But I move around a lot these days.'

'By sea?'

'Unfortunately.'

'You don't like sailing?'

'Not much. It's a sort of job for me. Deliveries and so on.'

'You mean delivering yachts?'

'Sometimes.'

Tom was intrigued, but at that moment a burly man who turned out to be Bob approached them, and the conversation was left hanging in a plane of cigarette smoke.

Bob Simmons, skipper and owner of Midday Gun, was a gruff former merchant seaman who had spent a redundancy payout on a forty-six foot yacht, and now trained novice sailors for a living. Bob held no affection for the sea; it was his workplace. Anyone who claimed to love the sea, he was fond of saying, obviously hadn't been on it much. In the summers he sailed on the Humber, up and down the East coast and across the North Sea to Holland, ticking off the miles his students needed for their qualifications. In the winter he took the yacht to the Mediterranean, usually assisted by Andy, a reliable old crewmate from his Merchant Navy days, and a fee-paying crew. Tom had chosen the trip more or less at random from the classifieds in Yachting Monthly. He wanted to be among strangers. He had a bundle of cash in his bag and no plans, and the leaving was more important than the destination.

Andy arrived at the Minerva, and then two locals, Suzanne and Alison, experienced sailors who had crewed with Bob before. 'Six. That's the lot of us, then,' announced Bob, looking around the table. 'Right, let's check what you've let yourselves in for. Three weeks of rum, sodomy and the lash. The yacht's all ready to go. We'll leave at high tide tomorrow morning, nice and early. Down the coast,' – he traced an invisible route on the table with his index finger – 'and maybe stop at Dover, then Cherbourg, round the corner to Bilbao, we could pop into Lisbon, see how we're doing, past Gibraltar, drop Ralph off at Marbella, then the rest of us go on to Mallorca. All happy with that?'

'Yes, Skipper.'

'We'll work in two watches. Three of us on each watch. Four hours on, four hours off. Tom and Ralph, you can be on the same watch, with Andy. He needs some muscle on deck to help him at his age. You three are Blue Watch. Suzanne and Alison, you can work with me. We'll be Red Watch. Agreed?'

'Aye Aye, sir.'

'Good. Whose round is it, then?'

Next morning Bob steered the yacht out of the great iron lock. He turned to port and hugged the north shore, out of the paths of the regal procession of cargo ships and barges plying their trade up and down the main channel. Tom looked back up the estuary to see the Humber Bridge draping its elegant arcs from shore to shore in a steel and concrete farewell. He pictured the tributaries beyond, the Trent and Ouse and Derwent weaving through the towns of his homeland, and wondered whether he would ever go back.

'Right, let's get these sails up,' said Bob, rubbing his hands together, and the crew went into action. A gull circled low overhead, brilliant white against the blue sky; the surface of the water was calm, and soon the yacht had settled into a beam reach, gliding steadily eastwards. Tom felt the pull of the sails and the surge of tide taking them towards the open sea, leaving behind the burdens of the land.

The Prime Meridian – zero degrees, the imaginary line which passes through Greenwich and from which longitude is measured around the globe – cuts across the Humber Estuary, north to south, at a point between Grimsby and Spurn Head, and as the yacht crossed from the Western hemisphere to the Eastern Tom pictured that perfect, cartographic line below the surface of the water, slicing the planet into segments like an orange.

Tom shared a cabin with Ralph. 'Bit cosy, isn't it?' Ralph said, as they settled in.

'Could be bigger. But it's a nice yacht.'

'I've been on better.'

'Like?'

'Aahh… a big cutter called Palomino. 110 foot. Fantastic yacht. Dark blue hull, teak deck. You might see her when we get to Marbella. What's the biggest you've been on?'

'This one.'

'You done much sailing?'

'A bit. Never this far, though. You?'

'Yeah, plenty. A few Atlantics.'

Long passages offer crewmates many hours and days to talk. People who board yachts as strangers are soon forced into intimacies, by proximity and adversity, and disembark as friends or enemies.

'What do you do for a living, Tom?' asked Ralph, on the second day, somewhere off Norfolk.

'At the moment, nothing. I'm an ex-pub landlord.'

'On the run?'

'I suppose so. If you want to be blunt.'

'So who's after you, back on the hated land?'

'Creditors, the taxman, some dodgy acquaintances. The police, probably. Oh, and a jealous husband.'

'Ah well. Worse things happen at sea.'

'What about you? What do you do?'

'Ah, bits and bobs,' said Ralph, staring at the horizon. 'Bits and bobs.'

In the depths of their second night at sea, Tom was woken by the sound of Ralph talking in his sleep in the bunk below. Tom sat up and could see the low coast of Kent in the moonlight beyond the hatch window. Ralph's sleep-talk grew louder: 'No. No. Help. Stop.' His arms began to thrash in a desperate, waving motion, and the words dissolved into primeval sounds. Tom reached down and shook Ralph by the shoulder.

'Ralph! Ralph! Wake up!'

'What? Uh? Oh fuck. Fucking hell.'

'It's alright, you were dreaming.'

Next day the two men were alone on deck, Ralph on the helm, Tom tidying ropes in the cockpit. The sails were trimmed to a gusting easterly breeze. Below in the galley, Skipper Bob was making tea.

'Sorry I woke you up last night,' said Ralph, gazing at the horizon.

'No worries. You get that often?'

Ralph paused. A tiny silence which, Tom thought, contained the true answer. 'No.'

'What were you dreaming about?'

'Dying.'

'How?'

'Drowning.'

Hundreds of liquid miles swept steadily beneath the hull. They passed through the sea areas of the shipping forecast: Humber, Thames, Dover, Wight. Conversations stretched over days, paused in the air, to be picked up hundreds of miles later. South of Portsmouth, Tom resumed the conversation with Ralph they'd started in the Minerva: 'What sort of delivery trips?'

'Sometimes new yachts. Sometimes moving yachts for rich owners who can't be arsed.'

Portland, Plymouth.

Off the coast of Brittany: 'Is there much money in it?'

'Delivery trips? Officially, no. But you can make other money out of it.'

Biscay, Fitzroy, Trafalgar.

Within sight of Lisbon: 'How?'

'How what?'

'How do you make other money out of delivery trips?'

'Ah, that. By taking certain goods from one place to another.'

'You mean smuggling?'

'If you want to be technical about it.'

'What sort of goods?'

'Mate, that would be telling.'

They barrelled into the Strait of Gibraltar in rising westerlies. Tom, Ralph and Andy came on watch at midnight. 'Hold on tight, it's choppy out here,' shouted Bob, handing over the helm to Tom. 'Steer seventy degrees.'

'Seven zero, skipper,' Tom confirmed.

Blue Watch clipped their harnesses to the guardrails and squinted like miners into the dark tunnel of the night. Black sea merged into black sky, obliterating the horizon. To starboard, lonely lights from tankers winked as they dipped behind steep waves, and to port the distant lighthouses of the Spanish coast beckoned. A double-reefed main and a small triangle of foresail were enough to drive the yacht briskly along, rolling and pitching as she went.

Helming was hard work. The boat would twitch one way, pushed by a wave, and Tom would steer her over the next, scalloping over an endless procession of white crests. He wrestled with the wheel as it yanked left and right, and soon his back muscles were sore from the struggle. His fingers stiffened with cold inside their leather gloves. Ralph sat in the cockpit, out of the wind and the spray, one glove off, prodding at buttons on the electronic chart. Conversation was difficult, drowned by the thumping of the hull and the whistling of the wind in the rigging. Up you come, Tom said out loud to the boat, as she recovered from each fierce gust. He felt her iron keel doing its work, sinking down again and again into the dark water, pulling the yacht back to the vertical.

The gale was blowing itself out and would be over in a few hours. Dawn would appear on the bow and there would be coffee and toast down below. By lunchtime they would moor in the safety of Marbella marina, and this night would seem like a bad dream.

'You ready to swap?' asked Ralph.

'Sure.'

Ralph unclipped his harness from the starboard shroud and moved to take the wheel; but a sudden rogue wave struck them on the aft quarter, the yacht lurched, and Ralph stumbled. He reached out with both arms for a handhold. He found none. Time seemed to stop.

Perhaps this was a hallucination. The sea does strange things to the mind's eye after a long trip. Solo circumnavigators report phantom crew aboard their lonely craft; other sailors see visions of land, of monsters and mermaids, cracks in the sky, great stone castle walls rising from the water.

But this nightmare was real. Tom's eyes flashed to Ralph's as they both saw, in a mental freeze-frame that each would keep until their dying moment, that Ralph was lost. His body jerked backwards across the low side of the pitching deck, over the guardrail and out of sight, into the deadly, broiling, black and lonely sea.

'MAN OVERBOARD!!' Tom howled, and the horror struck him like an axe. 'Man overboard!' A half-second of disbelief. A volley of shouts and furious activity in the dark. The three men on deck yelled above the howl of the wind.

'Start the engine!'

'Drop the sails!'

'Somebody point at him! Don't lose him!'

The yacht lurched broadside to the waves and its hull slapped violently into a slab of frothing water. The deck bucked like a rodeo horse. Sails flogged and cracked uselessly in the gale. The boom crashed from side to side, ropes whipped, winches span wildly. Alison, Suzanne and Bob scrambled into their lifejackets and rushed on deck.

'Get the boathook! Pass that rope!'

'Get on the radio! Mayday!'

Torrents of water sluiced along the gunwales, knocking the crew to their knees. Tom clung to the wheel. Salt water lashed his face and stung his eyes. This isn't real, he thought. This can't be happening. Not now, dear God. Not in ten-foot waves and a force seven, middle of a black night and twelve miles from the coast. Ralph could be dead already. Shit, shit, shit, we're losing him.

They searched for hours, motoring desperately back and forth across the same torrid patch of wet hell. A lifeboat and helicopter joined the frantic search, and the radio fizzed and crackled in different languages at maximum volume, but any hopes of finding Ralph alive were slim. Everyone knew it. The cold, thrashing sea would have killed him within minutes. The crew scanned the water with increasing desperation. In the morning the storm abated, the sun shone and the waves flattened, as if the weather gods were assisting the search, but the vast mirror of the Mediterranean offered up no clues. Evening fell and in the moonlight the silver sea glowed with malice. The search was called off. A hush fell across the deck and its haggard crew.

'Tom,' whispered Bob, 'see if you can find Ralph's passport. We'll need his next of kin.'

Tom retreated to the cabin, where Ralph's bunk lay dishevelled like a plundered grave. His scattered belongings seemed absurd now that they had outlived their owner. Tom picked them up reverently, like a museum curator handling ancient artefacts. He remembered as a schoolboy staring in awe at an Egyptian mummy in a glass case, and asking his teacher, 'Is this a real dead body?' Now he felt that same proximity to death.

Ralph's black holdall was wedged into a locker beneath his bed. Tom pulled it free, placed it on the bunk and unzipped it. The bag contained the yachtsman's usual bare necessities – shorts, hats, sunglasses – and beneath these, a large hardback book: The History of the Royal Ocean Racing Club. Odd, thought Tom. He hadn't seen Ralph reading it. He fanned the pages. Classic wooden yachts surged across the Solent in black and white, starched white commodores presented glittering trophies. Between the last pages was a reinforced manilla envelope emblazoned with the warning, 'Do Not Bend.' Tom gingerly pulled out its contents: a charcoal sketch of a naked male figure, walking towards the viewer with one hand outstretched. In one corner was an unmistakable signature.

Planking creaked under footsteps in the saloon. Tom slotted the sketch back into the book. From the other side of the closed cabin door Bob said, 'Tom, can you come up on deck? Crew meeting.'

The others had gathered in a tight circle out in the cockpit. Peaked caps and hoods shrouded the collective shock and grief.

'Right, I know this is going to be a bugger,' Bob said, 'but we're going to motor on to Marbella, and when we get there we'll have to answer a load o' questions. We've nowt to hide, we did everything right. It was just a tragic accident. Did anybody know where Ralph was planning to go after he left us?'

The crew looked at each other but no-one answered. 'Anybody know about 'is family? Where 'e lived? Anything?'

Blank faces. Ralph, it seemed, had taken the details of his secretive life with him to the seabed. 'Hmm,' said Bob, 'a man of mystery, then. Okay, everybody get some rest. Me and Andy will take us into Marbs. And if any of you want to jump ship and make your ways home when we get there, that's alright, I wouldn't blame you.'

They sailed on in silence, a ghost ship. Tom went back into his cabin and closed the door behind him. He took the sketch – a Picasso, a fucking Picasso - from Ralph's bag, and put it in his own, and in doing so, he realised, almost undoubtedly committed the offence of handling stolen goods. Ralph had been serious about smuggling. Deadly serious.

*

In Marbella marina Edward Lyons, silver-haired, tanned, straight-backed, stood in the sun on the long teak deck of his yacht and watched through binoculars the bustle around Midday Gun on a nearby pontoon. Uniformed customs officers, coastguards and policemen were questioning the crew, inspecting equipment and making notes on clipboards. A pair of police cars shimmered in the haze on the dockside.

'What do you think?' Lyons asked his bodyguard. He lowered his binoculars and squinted in the sunlight. 'Is Ralph there?'

'I haven't seen him.'

A policeman questioned Tom in efficient but fractured English. 'You shared a cabin with the man lost?'

'Yes.'

'You were at wheel when he fell?'

'Yes.'

'Did he say why he leaving yacht at Marbella?'

'No.'

'And you know not where he was going after this?'

'No. He kept himself to himself.'

'Por favor?'

'He was quiet. Didn't talk much.'

'Ah. I see. And you packed him away?'

'I packed his bag, yes.' Tom felt his pulse stop. The heat clamped him like a vice.

'Everything in the bag?'

'Yes, everything.' Tom wanted to plunge into the cool water below the pontoon. The mirror-shaded official stared at him for an inscrutable eternity.

'Gracias. You can go.'

The officials retreated one by one to make their reports. Tom made an excuse and walked to the end of the marina, where the mightiest yachts were proudly tied, and found the one he wanted: dark blue hull, teak deck. He stood at the foot of the gangplank and called out, 'Palomino! Anyone aboard?'

Edward Lyons emerged from the companionway. 'Yes?'

'I have a message from Ralph.'

More mirror shades, another pause. Then, 'Come aboard.'

Tom stepped out of his deck shoes, padded up the gangplank, and followed Lyons down the companionway into a sumptuous, air-conditioned saloon. Lyons eyed him suspiciously. 'Where is Ralph?'

'He's dead,' said Tom. 'Fell overboard. We couldn't find him.'

'That is tragic. I am sorry. Were you friends?'

'Not really.'

'But he told you about me?'

'No. He just mentioned Palomino.'

'What has happened to his... belongings?'

'I handed them over to the authorities.'

'Everything?'

'Not quite.'

'Then you still have something?'

'Yes. But maybe I should hand that over to them too.'

'I admire your bargaining technique.' Lyons took off his sunglasses and tugged at his neatly clipped white beard. 'One moment,' he said, and left the room. Tom cast a glance around the walls. Some of the paintings looked vaguely familiar. The bodyguard stood a few yards away, staring at Tom, unblinking. Beyond sliding glass doors two deckhands were vigorously polishing chromework.

Lyons returned with a handful of banknotes notes an inch thick. 'Allow me to make you a proposition. I was going to pay Ralph this' – he fanned the notes – 'for his delivery. I could pay you instead. When the item is in my hands.'

An hour later Tom was back aboard the superyacht. He handed the charcoal sketch to Lyons, who laid it carefully on the mahogany dining table and stooped to examine it with a magnifying glass. 'Thank you,' he said, not looking up. 'Study for Boy Leading a Horse, 1905. The finished painting is in the Museum of Modern Art in New York. Are you interested in art?'

'A little.'

'Are you interested in sailing?'

'Very.'

'I can always use yachtsmen.'

'I can always use money.'

'Then perhaps we can do business. Yachts are my favourite method of transportation. They leave little trace. Even the wake disappears quickly.'

'I understand.'

'We are leaving in the morning. I could use an extra pair of hands.'

'Where are you headed?'

'Antigua. We just sail south until the butter melts and then turn right.'

*

For two weeks the hull of Palomino sliced through Atlantic waves. The yacht was large enough to find privacy when Tom wanted it; he could lie on the foredeck, or sit in the air-conditioned saloon if the sun was too hot. Lyons had filled a floor-to-ceiling glass-fronted bookcase with carefully selected reading, from classic novels to business books, and a sailing shelf, of course; the epic sagas of Columbus and Magellan, the sea battles of Nelson and Drake, and memoirs of the solo circumnavigators – Slocum, Tabarly, Chichester, Knox-Johnston. Tales of disaster and survival. Donald

Crowhurst driven to madness and suicide by the lonely sea, the shipwrecked whaling crew of the Essex turning cannibal in their drifting lifeboat.

Late one evening, north of Cape Verde, Lyons appeared on deck with a coffee and a cigarette. Tom was reading by the light from the cabin. Lyons nodded towards his book and said, 'Have you been through the whole library yet?'

'I'm working on it.'

'Who have you got there?'

'Moitessier.'

'Went native, didn't he?'

'He's just made it round the world, but he's thinking about going round again instead of finishing the race. Don't spoil the ending.'

'There isn't one.' Lyons sipped from his china cup, his little finger cocked, and looked out at the vast, brooding ocean. 'He's probably still out there somewhere. Going round in circles, all alone, navigating by the stars.'

'I was just aiming at a star on my last watch. Didn't look at the compass for an hour.'

'Which star?' Lyons gazed up at the immaculate heavens.

'The bright one dead ahead, about thirty degrees up. It's bang on West.'

'That's Altair. In Aquila, the eagle.'

Tom rolled his head back and swept the universe. 'Wonder if there's anyone out there.'

'Maybe,' said Lyons, 'and maybe not.' He sipped the last of his coffee. 'Miraculous either way, don't you think?'

Two weeks later, as the sun began its daily descent ahead of the yacht, Antigua rose above the horizon. Tom, on the helm, was the first to glimpse the distant peaks, and kept the secret to himself for a while, until he was sure of what he saw; then with a shout of 'Land ho!' brought the crew grinning onto the deck.

Antigua has been journey's end for transatlantic voyagers since Columbus first paid a call. It sits near the tip of the Leeward Islands, a string of tropical paradises curving northwards from the coast of Venezuela towards Europe like a beckoning finger. Palomino was bound for English Harbour, a natural, high-sided bowl which for centuries has provided ships with shelter from high winds and hurricanes. But the price of the bay's refuge had often been death; in the Caribbean of yesteryear, yellow fever claimed more navy souls than war and the cruel sea. Nelson, stationed in Antigua for years among mosquitoes, disease and insufferable heat, considered the place an infernal hole.

Later in the afternoon, two miles off the island, Lyons took the wheel from Tom. The sea was calm, the sky immaculate blue. 'I'll do the last bit,' he said. 'If we hit the rocks it'll be my fault.'

'All yours.' The two men gazed at the high cliffs before them on the eastern side of the island, made rugged by the incessant assault of the trade winds and their waves. The rest of the crew were on the foredeck, staring at the unfamiliar land too, out of earshot.

'Have you decided what to do next, Tom?'

'Nope.'

'What are you after?'

'Oh, the usual stuff. Money. Adventure. Self-actualisation. A yacht like this one.'

'Laudable aims,' said Lyons. He paused, looked sideways at Tom for a moment, then continued. 'I have a few friends in high places here. I'm working on some projects and I need a replacement for Ralph.'

Tom took off his sunglasses.

'Are you offering me a job?'

'Perhaps. It wouldn't be much to start with. Running errands and suchlike. Security. But it could grow. Interested?'

Take it, whispered the dead, from the island's bloodthirsty earth: take it, you pass this way but once.

'Yes.'

'You'd have to be very discrete.'

'Like with the Picasso?'

'Yes,' said Edward Lyons, 'just like with the Picasso.'

The yacht continued its stately passage around the south-eastern peninsulas of the island, until a palisade of soft brown cliffs seemed to slide apart like the gates of a promised land. At a sign from Lyons the crew dropped the ocean-weary sails into concertinas on the booms. Mooring lines and fenders were hauled from the anchor locker where they had lain unused since Marbella.

Inside the harbour, squadrons of pelicans patrolled low over the sparkling water, and with a gentle splash an old man cast a net in a smooth arc from a bright yellow skiff. How vivid the solid features seemed, after weeks at sea; windblown palms on green hillsides, sun-blasted rocks, peeling emerald paint on clapboard sail lofts.

With the yacht safely moored, the crew settled at a table on a balcony bar overlooking the moorings. A waiter brought them cold bottles of beer. The bitter golden sparkle on Tom's tongue reminded him of England, a hundred years ago, a million miles across the sea. Palomino rested below, her elegant masts reaching for the cornflower sky, the sensuous sweep of her dark blue hull reflecting the smooth water.

The sun dipped in the west. Three flags above the Custom House hung motionless, and sweet smoke from a clay oven nearby carried the scent of frying fish into the still air. Tom leaned back and pictured himself from far above as a dot at the water's edge, the latest arrival in a colossal migration of people seeking better lives in the new world. He had crossed the wide Atlantic in the wake of long dead multitudes. The journey had weathered his stubble-peppered face; he was one of the Palomino crew now. He slowly put on his sunglasses, as if trying them on for the first time. Life would be different from now on. He'd keep himself to himself, just like Ralph had done. This was the other side of the world, beyond some invisible moral meridian, and there were projects requiring his discretion.

SANDRA ADAMS-WEST

I was born and raised in a town called Port Hueneme, California. I am a first-generation Californian, as my parents were born in the American South. I had an idyllic childhood, in a place where I could sunbathe on the beach in the morning and go hiking, mountaineering or skiing in the afternoon. I grew up among diverse cultures and, as part of a military family, spent a great deal of time at the former Pt Mugu Naval Air Station, which hooked me on my first love, fighter jets!

My first foray into writing started with a ten-page book report on Abraham Lincoln when I was in primary school. Total overkill, but I became enamoured with writing! Through my school years, I mostly wrote poetry. Upon completing high school, I did not think of becoming a professional writer, but I followed my heart and became a paramedic instead.

After a few years of this career, I left and followed another dream, to be a wife and mother. After my daughters started school, I went back to college and got a degree in journalism. I worked in newspapers alongside writing for theme park magazines, focusing primarily on the Disney parks.

In 1998, my daughters and I packed up and moved to the UK. I worked many years for a major British airline and put writing to one side. However, after my girls were grown, I decided to plunge back into writing and started my Master's degree at Hull to give myself the tools to become the writer I always wanted to be.

KARMA

'Damn, son. Y'all must have hit one hell of a buck to bust the front end like that.'

Fred, the head mechanic at the Big Cabin Truck Stop, stared in awe at the mangled front bumper and grill of an otherwise pristine semi tractor-trailer in his shop.

'Yep, 16 pointer, the state trooper said.' Tony Allen mumbled and looked dejectedly at the mechanic as his driving partner Clete Carter hovered nearby.

'Shoot, that'll fill up my freezer out back! You wanna trade that ol' deer for parts and labor on the truck?' asked Fred.

'How soon will the truck be ready?' Tony and Clete said in unison. Big smiles draped their faces.

Things were looking up.

A few hours later, Clete and Tony sat in the Big Cabin coffee shop, slurping back their third cup of coffee, waiting for Big Ernie, their beloved Peterbilt, to get fixed.

'You boys want a refill?'

Clete and Tony looked up at the waitress, hovering at the table, holding a steaming pot of the house full roast brew at the ready.

'Uh, why not, fill 'er up,' Clete said, 'and keep it coming!'

Callie Jones smiled down at the two men and said. 'Y'all the ones that took on the buck and lost?'

'That's us,' said Tony.

'Well, don't fret. Fred will get you back on the road in a hurry. The faster he gets you gone, the faster he can tell everyone how he brought down that buck! Mr God's gift to hunting he is not, but he likes to think he is in front of his buddies!'

'His secret is safe!' Clete said, 'I will tell the world he shot the buck, and we accidentally ran over his prize if he gets us back counting the mile markers on I-40 by noon like he promised.'

'If he said it, consider it done. Where you headed?' Callie asked

'Nashville!' Clete and Tony chimed in unison.

Callie sighed. 'I was headed there a few years back, was supposed to have a recording contract and everything. Left my old life behind and was on my way, but then EdEarl, the guy who discovered me, took it all away; he just squashed me down like a bug under his boot. So I ended up here in Big Cabin, with nothing to my name. Fred and his wife took me in, gave me a place to stay and a job here in the cafe. That was five years ago, and nothing has changed.'

'Why don't you move on?' Tony asked.

'Why bother? No point, who's gonna look at a girl from the middle of nowhere?' Callie asked.

'Whoa! Talk about cowinkidinks!' said Tony, 'Same sorta thing happened to me and Clete. Pull up a chair, honey. You ain't gonna believe this!'

Three years earlier…

Down on one knee, holding up the diamond chip ring set in 9-carat gold that had cost him his entire life savings, Clete looked up expectantly to Brandice, his girlfriend of 6 months. He'd asked her to marry him in front of all the customers and staff of The Pump, the swankiest waffle and chicken house in all of La Russell, Missouri. But, amidst the collective intake and holding of air, the silence was deafening. The assemblage waited with bated breath for the 'Yes' to be said and Boone's Farm Strawberry Hill Wine screw caps to be twisted.

Brandice's face was a mixture of disbelief and disgust, not what you would expect from a prospective bride to be, or a woman in love. She jumped out of her chair so quickly it tumbled back and hit a nearby table. Her mouth twisted into a snarl as she looked down with contempt at the man starting up at her with puppy dog eyes.

'What in the hell are you doing? I would never marry a pathetic moron like you,' she spat, 'I only dated you to get back at my ex-husband Dusty. I never want to see your ugly face again.'

She picked up her knockoff Shanelle handbag from the table and turned on her fake Prama heel, and walked out of his life forever. Clete dropped to the floor as though he had been punched in the gut, stunned by what had happened.

He heard the sympathetic murmurings of the people around him, getting louder and louder, a cacophony that threatened to drive him mad if he did not get away. So he bolted out the door and ran off into the warm and starry night.

Out of breath, he finally stopped running. Sitting down on a grass verge next to the quiet country road, his chest heaving from the strain, he pondered what to do. Going back now was out of the question.

He could not bear to be the subject of gossip around the county; everyone probably knew the whole story before he even hit the waffle house parking lot. He needed some distance. But how?

As he thought, he absentmindedly picked a daisy growing in the soft grass near his leg. He brought it up to his nose and instinctively inhaled its delicate fragrance. He twirled the daisy in his hand and thought how pretty it might have looked in Brandice's wedding bouquet. But then he remembered the looked of disgust she had given him and mentally slapped himself.

He started plucking the petals, and with each one, he uttered 'she loves me' or 'she loves me not' as each snapped from the head and drifted silently down to the ground. So intent was the daisy depetaling, he almost did not notice the lights of the Peterbilt 18-wheeler rumbling down the road. He stopped mid-pluck, looked up, and saw salvation was upon him.

The daisy went flying as Clete jumped up and stuck out his thumb. He'd hitchhike to anywhere. Anywhere far away from Brandice. Finally, the truck ground to a halt, the window opened, and a voice called out,' Need a ride?' Clete nodded affirmatively. 'Well, hurry up and hop in; I gotta this the load to Tulsa before tomorrow morning.'

Clete climbed up into the truck, settled into a soft leather seat, and then looked over at his new travelling buddy. 'Thanks for the ride. You sure are helping me out. I'm Clete.'

'Hey Clete, I'm Tony. Where you headed?' Clete sat for a few minutes and thought about the question. He finally answered, 'Anywhere but here, I don't care where.'

Tony looked back and forth between the road and Clete with a knowing eye. 'Girl did a number on you, didn't she?' Tony asked. Clete turned his face towards

Tony, and words tumbled out of his mouth, like a waterfall on Viagra.

When he stopped talking, Tony signed and said, 'I get it. I had it all once. A glittering career, a mansion in Malibu, ate at the best restaurants, went to all the 'in' parties, had a closet full of designer clothes. And my manager/girlfriend, Aria. She helped make me a star. She was my world.'

Lost for words, Clete stared at Tony. Finally, after a minute, he opened his mouth to speak, but Tony cut him off.

'I wanted to sing country music, get back to my Oklahoma roots, but she said I needed to stay relevant to the masses. I HATE POP. I only did it to please her. I decided to dump her and do my own thing. But before I could do it, Aria found out; she went crazy with a capital C. Long story short, I was dumped by the record company and kicked out of my house and my life. Now here I am, driving a truck at 3am.'

Clete said, 'Wow, same for me, without the career, house, clothes and parties. But, hey, I got a cool idea! We should work together, driving trucks and writing good country music!' Tony nodded enthusiastically, and they got down to business.

Six months later....

'Next on KRAP's HonkyTonk HoeDown, we bring you the newest country sensation, the Cletone Truckers, and their new Number One hit, 'Dumped!' So take it from me, JD the DJ, all us good old boys can Ra-late!!'

I gave up my booze, my ciggies and lunch
To get you a ring that cost a whole bunch
You tossed me away like yesterday's trash

Then you took my house and stole all my cash

You acted so sweet; I loved you so true

But you done turned into a haggy old shrew

Callie's gaze moved back and forth between the two men, her eyes wide and her mouth agape.

'OMG, You're the Cletone Truckers! I can't believe I am meeting you guys. And your story, how wonderful. Well, not wonderful; you guys got dumped and lost everything. That sucked. But I want to record music and sing all the time. And to get married. And have a mansion in Malibu.'

Callie glanced up at the ceiling as her eyes became dreamy, thinking of her chance to be in the limelight.

'Hang on, girl, it's not all Malibu, mansions and happy endings. We got lucky. Once. You have to keep at it, or you lose it again just as quick.'

'Did you lose it again? I mean, you guys are driving trucks.'

'Not because we have to, but because we want to. We do our best writing when we're driving!' said Clete.

'The open road, the small towns, the country going by, it all tells a story. And we make that story into music. Food for the soul. Not to mention our stomachs!' Tony laughed.

'Really, it's that simple?' Callie asked.

'Well, no, but when you love to do something, it can come easier than fixing a truck or pouring a cup of coffee!' Tony pointed to his cup and smiled.

Callie giggled. 'Be nice, or it will be in your lap!' She got up and went to the coffee machine to start a fresh pot, then returned to the booth where Clete and Tony were sitting.

'So, Callie, what happened to you, if you don't mind me asking,' said Clete.

'Ah, you guys know the story. A girl likes to sing and tries to make a few bucks in the bars and clubs. Girl gets sweet-talked by a smarmy guy in with a nice bolo tie and rodeo buckle; a girl can't see the forest for the trees. The girl gets used, the girl gets dumped, the girl ends of in the middle of nowhere. And her dreams die. It all started to go downhill when I was waiting for a train...'

Five years earlier...

The 9:20 was late again. Just like it always was. You could set your watch by the lateness.

Callie glanced at her Timex and signed. She would never be able to hit the big sale in Little Rock at this rate, not for the good bargains anyway. Just like her life. She always got the leftovers, what no one else wanted. Everyone always said - you will never get the best, be happy with the worst; it's all you deserve. That was all anyone like her ever got.

But this time, it was to be her last bargain sale. She'd been scouted by EdEarl DuBois of JimBob, EdEarl & Mo's BBQ, the best honky-tonk in the county. They were going to fix her up with a recording contract. She could leave Cooperman's General Store in Hominy Corners behind and never look back. She was off to Nashville, and she was going to be the toast of the town. EdEarl told her so.

Her ears perked up when she heard the stationmaster's voice over the loudspeaker. 'Sorry folks, train's been delayed. Hit a cow at Miller's Creek. Dunno when that mess'll get cleaned up. Y'all can wait over to Miss Bessie's café. I hear she just made a passel of cornpone and weasel stew. Yum-Yum!'

Callie's stomach retched at the thought of weasel anything. It reminded her of Beauregard, the weasel who stepped all over her heart to take up with the town tramp, Sue Ellen Sanderson.

I am not hanging around this dump one more minute, she thought. She buttoned up her threadbare coat, picked up her valise, and walked out into the morning sunlight.

She walked about a mile, past the old feed store and flour mill, up the on-ramp to the interstate. The road to her destiny. She waited a few minutes, and up the ramp came a sleek blue eighteen-wheeler – a Peterbilt hauling John Deere tractors. She thought there might be a song in there somewhere, a Peterbilt on the open highway bringing the farmer his John Deere. Top 40 material! The Hominy Corner's Dolly Parton was on her way.

'That eighteen-wheeler blew a tire and got towed here to Big Cabin, the middle of Nowhere, Oklahoma. The tire got fixed, but while I was in the ladies' room, the trucker left. Everything I owned but my purse and the clothes on my back went with him. Fred's wife found me crying at a table, and they gave me a fresh start. It's not what I wanted or what I dreamed up. But life goes on. And any place that isn't Hominy Corners is better than nowhere.'

'Wow, Callie, that is tough. You have not had it easy,' Clete said, 'But what about EdEarl and the recording contract?'

'After I calmed down a bit, I asked Fred if I call borrow his phone, and I called EdEarl. It turns out he was full of crap. He was never giving me a contract; he did not know anybody anywhere. Said the only thing he wanted to do was screw me, and he didn't get that. He found someone new, who sings while he screws her, literally.'

Clete choked on his coffee and Tony's jaw when slack. They looked at each other and then back at her, speechless. She was so deep in the story; she did not appear to notice their surprise.

'I don't even want to think where I'd be if it weren't for Fred and his missus. They showed me what was important in life. I just hope someday I can show them how grateful I am.'

The bell on the coffee machine dinged, and the smell of freshly roasted Roadhouse Special filled the air. Callie got the pot and filled Clete and Tony's cups to the top. Neither one could speak; both had their heads down, unable to look her in the eye. Callie carried on like she was having a normal conversation and focused her gaze on Tony.

'I know the story of Clete, but you are still a mystery. What happened out in Malibu?'

His head jerked up, and he looked her straight in the eye.

'Huh? What?'

'Malibu, Tony. Tell me what happened.'

Tony shook his head as if to clear his mind. It was pretty obvious Callie was laying her story on the line, getting rid of her demons. Maybe he should too.

May 2011…

Tony reclined in his chair under a blue and white umbrella that matched the nearby pool and hot tub tile.

The summer sun burned bright. The 2010 Grammy Awards were a month away, and he was up for a handful of the gongs. The stack of publicity photos in his hand awaited his attention, but his eyes wandered to the calm ocean view before him.

He should be feeling on top of the world. He was a star, the toast of Tinseltown, a country boy who made it big. He had all the trappings of celebrity, a vast estate on a Malibu bluff overlooking the Pacific, a fleet of flash cars, money in the bank. He had it all.

Life had been happy in Kiowa, Oklahoma, the little town on Highway 69. He grew up there, along with the love of his life, Sissy June. He wanted to settle down, have some kids and a farm. He played the guitar with a band on Saturday nights down at the VFW and sang a bit with Sissy, who fronted the band. He wrote songs for her while on his breaks at the feed mill. Eat, work, write, love. That was all he truly wanted.

Sissy June had other ideas. She wanted to be an actress and a singer, like Dolly or Cher. And California held the key to unlock her dreams. Tony did not want her to leave, but she made a deal with him. Five years to follow her dream, and then, no matter what, she would come home. Mr and Mrs Tony Allen would live happily ever after.

Tony was so in love with Sissy June he followed her west. He figured he could get a job, and she could pursue her dream. They would be together. It worked for a bit. The two of them ever sang at a country bar in the city called Home Fires.

Hollis Hart, the owner of Home Fires, was also the owner of CoPop Records, an up and coming label that was taking the West Coast by storm. He had been listening to Sissy June and Tony for weeks, and he was looking at a star.

The trouble was, it was not Sissy June he was looking at; it was Tony. Hollis was determined to drag the county out and put the pop in. Within a few short months, Donny Starlite was born and took the world by storm.

Sissy was furious; how dare Tony steal her dream. She plotted and schemed, determined to cash in on Tony. Sissy June became Aria Soule, popstar manager extraordinaire by day and glamourous arm candy of Donny Starlite by night. She became a legend in the music world, never settling for less than the best, and propelling Donny to superstardom. And she never let Tony forget it.

Tony enjoyed his life at first, but the shine of stardom faded very quickly. He was singing, but not his songs; if he was going to sing, he wanted to sing his music, his way. Control became his enemy; every move was executed to the second; Aria made sure of that. She picked out his clothes, what he ate, what he sang, who he met. Aria became his lover, but not his love. He wanted privacy. He wanted his life back, and he wanted his Sissy June.

Aria made it clear to him yesterday, Sissy June was a memory, nothing more. Aria was everything, and without her, he was nobody. His dreams were dashed, like the waves pounding on the shore below him.

He looked down at the photos in his hand, waiting to be signed by Donny Starlite, and suddenly it became clear. This facade, the illusion. That was never his life. No matter which way he sliced it, he was country, not pop. No one, not even Aria, would ever stop him again.

He got up and walked to the edge of the cliff and threw the photos into the sea. It was over. His life was going to be his own.

'I was just going to walk away. I went back to the house to call Hollis and tell him just that. Hollis pleaded with me to reconsider, to come in and have a talk. I said no, I was packing up and going back to Oklahoma. He must have called Aria because about 15 minutes later, she came running in like a Texas tornado, told me I was through, she was going to ruin me. And she did.'

Tony took a deep breath and looked at Callie and Clete, who stared at him, shocked.

'And here we are, two truck drivers and a waitress, in nowhere Big Cabin, Oklahoma,' Tony said.

Callie smiled. 'If this is not a Nashville sensation waiting to happen, I don't know what is!'

Clete jumped up! 'Damn, son, hitting that deer is gonna be the best thing that ever happened to us three!' And they got down to business.

Two years later…

'And now, making their first appearance here at the Grand Ole Opry, are Miss Callie Jones, Clete Carter and Tony Allen. A few years back, this trio burst onto the country music scene out of nowhere, as Callie and the Cletones!' said Blaine Simmons, host of the show

'The boys formed the Cletones several years ago, and they captured our hearts with their hit single, Dumped! Now they have teamed up with Callie and have become one of Nashville's most successful new acts ever seen.

'Please help me welcome this year's County Music Association winners of the Vocal Group, Song, Single and Album of the year. Singing their award-winning song Karma, give it up for Callie and the Cletones!!!'

We decided, over coffee and lunch
Karma would mess you up a whole bunch
Now Aria is back as Sissy June trash
Brandice is dead broke and begging for cash
EdEarl has learned, finally it's true
Karma's a bitch; she's not an old shrew.

EPITAPH

Dear Diary

Death. What a dreary word. We all have to go some time, but why does it have to be such a downer? We can't escape it; the Grim Reaper has our names and dates in his planner. Just like Santa has us on his list or our Maker has us in his Book of Judgement. I would be more worried about which side of Santa's list I am on. However, the world's preoccupied dodging the burial bullet, and that's gonna keep the wolves from my door.

Here I am, a wannabe Clancy, stuck finding inspiration on old gravestones to write on new ones. I should be hanging out with Kim and Kanye rather than whipping up the last goodbye of some cadaver headed for Heaven or Hades. But hey, a girl has to earn a little coin somehow, right?

You ask, who was my first cadaver? Richard Rios, husband of Mary-Lou, ardent Democrat and Trump trasher; my kind of guy. Mary-Lou wants something epic. How can I get epic on a gravestone? Think I might need to go look for inspiration at the bottom of a glass of chardonnay. I am doomed. But a job is a job, so I had to get this right.

Digging around, I found some excellent epitaphs out on the internet for inspiration. One said something like if the top politicians and clergy got off a train in heaven, then the guy was bound to get off at another station! One said, 'Cause of death: Reaganomics'. I almost spit my wine out at that one. The one that pulled at my heartstrings said, rather poignantly, 'Black Male'. How apropos that is today in this screwed up world? But they sure have given me food for thought.

And I never knew that my new occupation was such an old one; it goes back to the Egyptians. LOL! Here lies the great King Tut, stuck in an eternal rut! I crack myself up sometimes! What if old Bill Shakespeare wrote his own? I imagine he would have said,' Here lieth me, Fiddle-de-de.' Droll, very droll. Guess I better not quit the day job. Oh, wait…

OK, back to Richard. He obviously hates Trump; maybe I can use a type of Reaganomics thing somehow. But right now, I need some shut-eye. Later, tater!

10 Feb 2020

Dear Diary

So, inspiration struck, and I came up with what I thought was a beauty of an epitaph, but I was a bit leery of showing it to Mary-Lou. I did not want to insult the memory of Richard, but I could not think of any better way to show his disdain for Trump for the world to see today and forever!

She came to the office about noon, she was teary as she sat down, and I was beginning to question my judgement, not to mention my sanity. I told her I had written only one epitaph so far, but maybe this was not the time to show it to her. She held out her hand, and I handed her the page upon which I had written the following:

> Richard Alejandro Rios
> 04 Jun 1940 – 25 Jan 2020
> God is my hero, not Donald Trump
> He put Satan right into a slump
> I love my country; she is class
> But old Donnie boy, forever an ass.

A sharp intake of breath was followed by complete silence. I knew my career was over before it started. And I was right; it was.

In the end, Mary Lou loved it, and Richard got his epitaph. My employer, not so much. But Richard and I got to stick it to Trump, always and forever! Win-Win!

LALI ASRATOVA

It all started long ago. I aspired to create something magical, like the stories I'd read in books from all over the world. Like the tales I'd heard from people while moving with my family from place to place across former USSR.

Born in Georgia and raised in Moscow where I devoured the classics of Tolstoy, Turgenev, Dostoevsky and many more in Russian. That's when I picked up a pen, humbly trying to emulate their greatness! I occasionally dabbled with romances and crime stories at medical school and through my PhD. But I only started writing regularly after moving to London, marrying and having my son. A stream of poems about brushing teeth and potty time, brave animals and daring children came along.

I have just settled back in the UK with my family, having lived for a decade in Hong Kong. Recently, I successfully completed a Masters in Creative Writing at the University of Hull. And that's how the journey concludes to this Anthology.

The story of *Anaid and Davit* describes the not-quite-romance between two young people in post-war Georgia. Where 'proper behaviour', dictated by strict rules of the patriarchal society, forbade and shamed strong sensual feelings in women, forcing them into weak and passive beings.

No More Play! No More Toys! is a story for middle graders of evil and bravery and friendship, where the children try to save play time and rid 'the Evil Man'.

NO MORE PLAY! NO MORE TOYS!

Then came the day when everything changed.

The notice on the board in giant letters read: 'NO MORE PLAY! NO MORE TOYS! THOSE WHO BREAK THE RULES WILL BE PUNISHED!'

The Evil Man in black stood in the middle of the Great Hall of the Orphanage. Too lofty and too scraggy, with lanky legs and elongated arms, a skeleton clad in black, oozing a revolting smell of rotten cabbages.

He told the matrons, the teachers and two hundred children that to play or to keep a toy is against the law.

"All toys must be collected and burned immediately. Anyone who tries to hide a toy will be cast out to the streets!" he said, his spectacles gleaming at the end of his long, bony nose.

A red-faced orphanage Director stood like a frozen puppet, not a word came out of his mouth.

The Music Teacher was angry. "Sir, music instruments are not toys. You ordered them to be removed. May I ask why?"

"No, you may not! Music is bad for children. It distracts them from important work. And that's that!" the Evil Man said, with a smirk on his thin lips.

The English Teacher's voice stuttered, "W-w-what about story books, sir? F-folktales and fantasies …"

"Burn them!" the Evil Man roared and his voice echoed through the Orphanage.

The Evil Man left, his black robes flapping and thrashing about like the wings of an ugly bat. When the doors shut behind him, everyone in the Great Hall let out a sigh of relief.

The Director came to life with his arms waving in the air like a windmill on a windy day. He waved the children to return to their rooms, waved the matrons to attend to the children, and waved the teachers to get to their work.

The Geography Teacher was puzzled. "What about globes, maps, models?"

"I don't know!" snapped the Director.

The PE Teacher stepped forward. He was very scared but pretended not to care. "How should I train children if I cannot use a ball? Everyone loves football, netball ..."

"I don't know!" snapped the Director again. "We should all think of a new plan for lessons."

The PE Teacher seemed to deflate like a stabbed balloon.

Everyone was scared. No one, absolutely no one wanted to be cast out to the streets.

Hundreds of boys and hundreds of girls left alone in two long dark rooms, divided by a long narrow corridor, were scared too. Worried matrons forgot to give them their dinner, so hungry children went to bed with bellies making loud noises. They could not sleep because they were missing their toys and books with kind tales and bright pictures: their bulldozers, excavators, dolls, balls, fairy-tales and fables were burning in the fire in the back yard. The glow of the big fire was scary too.

Seb lay in his bed feeling sad and all alone in the world. He was missing his teddy bear that he had hidden in a hurry under the stairs. It was dangerous! He knew deep down he was too old to play with soft toys. But his teddy was the only memory he had of his parents. He didn't understand what was happening. Why did they take his old building blocks and his ball away? He pleaded with them, but it didn't help. The sadness was heavy, so heavy, and hurting inside him. He remembered that he had already felt like this before. But that time it was his parents he was missing. A grief, bigger than he could hold inside, spilled out and turned into a hot rage against the Evil Man in black with spectacles for taking away what little he had.

I will not let him take away my teddy bear! he thought. I must hide it better, before someone finds it.

Seb listened to the silence in the room for a long time, and then got up, put on his pants, t-shirt and sneakers. He didn't forget to tie his shoelaces with a 'loop, swoop and pull' knot, his mom had taught him when he was five. He took a deep breath, slowly opened the door and stepped into the long, dark corridor.

The Master Clock in the Great Hall struck midnight.

Seb's foot met the ground and the old floorboards let out a tired groan.

"Oh no!" he gasped and froze, goggle-eyed. His heart beat like a blasting drum, sure to wake everyone up, any time now.

He listened … strange … no hurrying footsteps. Nothing stirred. Only 'thump-thump-thump' of his heart. He counted to a hundred, lifted up the other foot and was about to place it on the wooden floor, when a clear voice said, "What are you doing?"

Seb's whole body jerked violently. He spun round expecting dragons or worse – the Evil Man himself.

Instead, a round face, sprinkled with masses of golden freckles and a pair of large, laughing eyes stared at him.

"Timmy! You scared me!" Seb hissed.

Timmy stumbled out of bed and hurried towards him, upsetting shoes and slippers as he went.

"Where are you going?" he whispered.

"Go back to bed. I have something very important to do," said Seb.

Timmy looked straight into his eyes. "I can help."

Secretly, Seb was glad that Timmy was up. "Right … you better put your clothes on then!"

Seb waited for Timmy to dress and remembered the first time they met three years ago.

That spring, after the crash killed his parents, Seb was brought to the Orphanage in a big black car accompanied by a tired matron and a kindly policeman. He was afraid of life in a strange house full of strangers. That first day, he sat on the bench next to a little boy, who cried big, burly sobs. That was Timmy. Seb patted his shoulders and told him funny stories. He taught Timmy the "1-2-3-4, I declare a thumb war" game.

After that, he felt a tiny bit better, and a tiny bit braver, and a tiny bit in charge. He was changing things around him, a tiny bit. That was BIG! They had been inseparable since then.

The memory of that day put a smile on Seb's face. "Follow me!"

They entered the dark corridor, Seb first, Timmy right behind. This time, the creaky floorboards kept silent.

The air was cold here and alive with strange sounds. Seb could swear he heard a voice whispering: 'Stop! Go back!'

Fear told them lies and made them see things that were not real. The gleaming spectacles of the Evil Man seemed to be everywhere, in dark corners, behind the furniture, gazing at them through the windows and from the portraits on the walls – sitting on the noses of the former directors of the Orphanage.

Keeping along the wall, the boys crept to the main stairs and climbed down.

They reached the back of the stairs and stopped. There, behind the steps, near where Seb had hidden his teddy, was a door. This door was never, never opened! But tonight it stood ajar, with a strip of light leaking out from under it.

"Timmy, we've got to hurry! Someone's there!" Seb faced the back of the stairs and ran his fingers along the steps where they met the wall, "I left it here, in the corner." He reached forward and his fingers felt the comforting softness of his teddy. "I've got it!"

He turned clutching the bear to his chest and gasped.

Timmy was gone and an ever-so-slight whiff of cabbages lingered …

To be continued …

ANAID AND DAVIT

I Anaid

As she tilted towards the turbid brown of the grimy water beneath the banks of the river Kura, her whole life flashed before her eyes.

She watched herself on the promenade. A dark shade on the grey of a nasty day. The thick river below called her. The pull was powerful; she couldn't resist. Even the ugly colours of its water weren't sufficiently repulsive to deter her yearning.

Climbing up onto the parapet, each move awkward and uncertain, a thought of her clever choice wearing sneakers stood out in the clutter of her brain. She saw herself smirk and lean towards the murky depth.

There the time stood still and she was off stirring the past.

Sunday in Avlabari, the oldest area of Tbilisi. Unending rows of washing hung on lines, stretched along wooden loggias of two-story buildings nursing many homes, centred around a communal yard.

She and her beloved granny, Tatik, lived in an apartment on the first floor.

The neighbours were busy cleaning and washing. A great day for her and the other children to run around and through the long lines of laundry that served perfectly for their games of hide-and-seek and ring-a-levio. Adults shooed the noisy friends away, before exchanging their secrets for ridding the toughest stains and recipes of scrumptious dishes.

The boisterous bustling Armenian district. It watched and cared for her and the other children, looking after their every need. No child could have ever been in danger or lost there. That was what the neighbourhood was about. Weddings, birthdays and any kind of anniversaries were enough for everyone to set long tables with wooden benches in the common yards and celebrate together.

In the mornings, with no bathroom or boiler, Tatik would heat up some water for her to wash in the aluminium tub. Then, delicious pancakes stuffed with potatoes or cheese or meat were served for breakfast, aided by a glass of home-made lemonade.

In the evenings in their living-dining-bedroom, she would watch her granny play lotto with friends using cherrystones for betting. Endless chatting and countless cups of tea chimed and chinked about the room, rocking lazily to and fro. Queries of her little achievements at school, in sports and music were the first to air. Sometimes, they would fry a slice of ryebread on the poky iron stove fed by chopped wood. A dash of salt and it was delicious.

The infinite sea of the rounded terracotta tiles of the roofs stretched forever along the left bank of the Kura, behind her window. And swallows, birds in tailcoats and a rusty bow tie, were a usual sight in spring, flying back to their loggia weaving nests on the joint of a ceiling and a wall. The cacophony of the parents feeding their offspring with juicy worms were the delight of most of her mornings.

The spring she and Tatik moved in with her parents and siblings, the swallows left the neighborhood, never to return. A young neighbor tired of their trill and tweets in the early mornings, crashed the newly built nests using his mother's wooden mop.

In a trice, the scene changed, as if the angle of a camera altered, and its eye confronted another image, projecting her sitting at the table.

Her dearest friend's 16th birthday party – Eva invited her girlfriends with a scandalous yet firm instruction to bring their elder brothers, who in their turn tagged along a few friends, placing a chief total of boys around the table. Chairs and stools were borrowed from the neighbours to sit the guests. It was rather a daring party for a patriarchal neighbourhood of Georgia in the 1950's, ruled by a strict set of social conducts.

The buzz and excitement of young people of the opposite sex who against all odds found themselves thrown together at a jolly celebration, echoed through the watchful neighbourhood for many months to come.

Then she was singing for them. Her voice had no barriers – everything else she did was carefully tailored to the strict measurements of a 'proper' behaviour required of a young girl. But her voice was free. Free to flow without any restrictions, arresting and imprisoning everyone in that room. She knew of the power of her singing and exulted in it.

She sang her last song and then and there … she felt it – a presence of some sort, like a quantifiable current around her. She looked for an account, a cause and found its source – an aquiline face and a pair of eyes, the greenish-brown of the river Kura, watched her intently, drunk her in, and claimed her for themselves. It was terrifying yet liberating. A tiny entity of an unknown origin grew inside the centre of her being, spreading and eating into her flesh, into the tiniest elements of her physical form. It filled her up with petrifying pleasure that weighed her body, shackling her limbs, stripping her completely of the awareness of any other being in the room, leaving her helpless and hopelessly famished for more.

A fear, an absolute fear of such a huge and overwhelming, yet alien desire paralysed her, disabling her will, stripping her of any other choice but to deny it. She was a mouse watched by a cat. And as a mouse she ran and hid herself … for weeks – his fiery eyes watching her. In her struggles to escape, to forget them, she thought even more about him and remembered seeing him at times when the war was still on and thriving, and people were drained and starving. He would walk through their street on the way home, a mesh bag thrown over his back filled with a few carrots and onions. Tatik said once that he was earning three hundred grams of meat weekly as his wages. It was then 1944, he was fourteen and meat was an almost forgotten luxury.

Despite her girlfriends' persuasions to meet with him and see if she may like him, she never gave in. Tatik told her that his sister came and asked if he could meet her. Her answer was the same: 'No'.

Another scene emerged from the debris of her memories. Not of her drunkard husband she wheedled into a divorce, or her hateful mother-in-law, who poisoned every minute of her married life, blaming her for being barren. Not even of her parents or sisters … didn't she love them? Were they not important at the time of her ending? She had no clue, no knowledge why. She was powerless to choose, as if an ingenious and prevailing director programmed the focuser and lenses of a silent camera, prioritising just on the clarity of the image.

She saw herself walking on the street, a shopping bag in her hand and a few coins in her pocket, to buy milk and a loaf of bread, and hurry back home. She and Tatik were soon to leave the neighbourhood for good and move to her parents' house on the other side of Tbilisi. All the furniture and most of Tatik's belongings were given away and only some of their clothing remained unpacked.

The cheerful morning rain had rustled through the streets and the air was crowded with a jolly chirping of the sun-up birds, a fresh 'after-the-rain' scent and a sweet aroma of sycamore trees. She reached Avlabari Lane and a whiff of mint, basil and of freshly backed shoti steered her towards the vegetable market with the delicious bakery, celebrated by the whole city. The smell of home.

The soft drowsiness of the morning hour was swiftly withdrawn by a jolly tune that seemed to travel down from Lagodekhi Street towards her and a few other pedestrians: some with fishing rods heading for the Metekhi bridge, others with shopping bags heading in the opposite direction.

A luxurious car approached her and slowed down with *him* at the steering wheel. She stopped, stunned by his presence and the fact that the music was certainly coming from his car. Avoiding his stare, her eyes wandered through the interior of the vehicle. There was no one else and nothing playing the tune. A gathering crowd on the street was also confused. Hand-wired-gramophones were very rare, and only 'rich and famous' were in ownership of those machines. Years after, she learned from Eva that he hid a friend with a pathéphone in the boot of his car and the instruction to play until told otherwise. She smiled at the memory.

He was always the talk of the whole Avlabari. At 1.7 meters, he was among the shortest of the young men population, yet he had the tallest name for himself at nineteen, and everyone, even 'elder and wiser' would come to seek his advice. He knew how to stop fights and resolve arguments, how to organise people, young and old. At the age of twenty, he opened his first factory producing steel rods for supporting grapevines, decreasing the breakage and increasing the country's grape production twofold.

He drove further and disappeared around the corner. The melody clung in the air for a few more seconds refusing to follow, then dissolving into a nullity, as did he.

She never saw him again.

But the passion he awoke in her heart although petrifying, never ceased to exist, depriving her of any chance to truly love another, to build a happy future with anyone else.

A total remorse and an absolute capitulation to it struck her hard.

What if? What if she had met with him? What if Tatik and her had stayed for a few more months?

A certainty of a different life filled with love and realised dreams presented itself.

A low, animal growl escaped her scowling lips as she tilted towards the ugly colors of the waters below.

"Davit …"

II Davit

Drop the suitcase at the hotel room, a quick shave and I'm out at the tram stop across the street, with a confectionery store at the corner. Each time its door opens, the tantalizing fragrance rich in sugar blasts out and spreads over the streets picking up speed as it moves downhill, cupping the neighbourhood in a cloud of vanilla-cardamom aromas.

The nearing tramcar, in cream-red with cables on the roof, reminds me of a snail with tentacles clinging to an electric wire... has the same movement and pace too – it glides unhurriedly along the rails, then stops. The doors fold up like an accordion letting the crowd through.

I find a seat and settle in. The tram starts off and moves leisurely, stopping now and then and panting heavily. Down the street, around the corner, along the Rustaveli Avenue lined with sycamore trees on both sides. On and on, passing the Old Town, with pitched roofs of brown, green, and dirty-white tiles. The dim daylight in the window shades the houses into undefined blue, yellow and green. Up and across the Bridge of Love and down to Avlabari station. From here I walk.

It is Sunday in Avlabari. It welcomes me with a bracing wind, lines of flapping laundry, clapping and cheering sycamores, ticking and chattering swallows, and a gallimaufry of Armenian-Russian interchanges.

Then comes the smell of 'hashi' – my Aunty Amalia's prize Sunday special that required her to stay overnight simmering cattle tripe to ready for our early morning treat.

She served it with an ample amount of garlic and, for the adults, a shot-glass of vodka.

Cobbled streets take me around my childhood neighbourhood pausing here and there for a short story narration by people I long knew.

I talk to Granny Maniko on Tsiskari Street. Perched on a low stool in front of a small table with a large aluminium bowl, brimmed with sunflower seeds she trades for a few cents per small glass. Everyone in the neighbourhood comes to buy from her as the quality is superb – Granny Maniko fries her seeds with a serene care that seasons each kernel with a unique flavour and dresses it in a crispy and shiny shell.

Sunflower-seed-munching tradition is a national pastime in Georgia. My friend Zaza was the champion at the disassembling of kernels for he had perfect hand-tongue-tooth coordination.

It seems Granny Maniko has on the same dress she wore twenty years ago, covering her from neck to the tips of her toes, yet a little off-colour and somewhat looser. Her face also the same – kind and smiley, yet different – netted with coarse folds and deep wrinkles, inscriptions of love and loss.

"Good morning!"

"Barev dzes!" Granny Maniko has always mixed Armenian and Russian more than anyone in the area, no doubt to make her sense to people. "You've grown strong, me mard." It means 'the Man'. She has called me that name since I was four. I 'rescued' her by merely opening a vehicle's back door and offering my hand for her to climb out of the family car. She was stuck inside, unable to push its handle open … her son-in-law and daughter left forgetting about her. I happened to be around.

Granny Maniko's hands are always busy. She forms a cone out of old newspaper and fills it up with seeds. I stand enthralled by the tittering and giggling din of the rushing kernels.

We exchange coins and I continue my journey.

I haven't walked along these streets for over twenty years. Past the vegetable market, up Avlabari Turn, down Avlabari Lane and to the house I grew up in.

A poky old building with a tilted wooden balcony of uncertain colour looks so much smaller than I remember, and a little tired, yet steadfast.

I was the eldest of four siblings brought up in this house. We were close, watching over each other. I remember every time a kindly neighbour offered me a lollipop or a cookie, I would ask for three more. That was why they called me 'Three-More'.

Curving and coiling, climbing up and down, the narrow streets formed a loop that served as a perfect playground for us. We would play there after school with other kids: hide and seek, tag, blind man's bluff, racing, robbers, you name it. And often make toys ourselves for the games, cutting and carving sticks into dolls and daggers.

During the war, we would build pistols and machine guns from old boards to play soldiers. Nobody would agree to be a German soldier, this role was assigned to trees or lamp posts.

Ball games were our absolute favorite. True, we didn't have a real ball, but we could make one from old rags, twisting them tightly and tying them with a knot. Such balls did not jump very well but were good enough for us.

I used to make the best balls in the area, until my mum found out the method I used. We had a small hosiery machine stuck at the back room in the house, for knitting wool and cotton stockings. My mum would weave long threads into tubes, then sew a toe end and pack a pair for market sale. I would 'borrow' a tube like that and stuff it with some wool from my mattress to form a sphere and tie it with a rope. Such a ball was light and bounced so much better.

Those were happy days. Those were days before I met her.

Even now, my pulse races when thinking about her and orchestrates a release of firecrackers within me.

It was April 25th, 1950 when I saw her for the first time, at a birthday celebration I was invited to by mere chance. Well, I'd seen her many times before in the streets and shops, but that day I truly saw her as she was, and my heart was lost forever.

Looking back, I can now understand the mechanics of what happened then. She sang and her voice took me on a journey.

At the beginning, there was nothing unusual, just the unsteady flickering and trilling of the lights in the room. I didn't see it coming. It sneaked up silently … the shy, tender tremor of her voice tiptoed softly to my eyes and ears, crawled through my skin and inside.

It sprouted into a slight throbbing, thumping into a rhythmic beat, vibrating musically into my being. It engulfed my muscles, organs, crept inside my cells and reached the nuclei.

With a powerful thrust, it divided the atoms and sent my elements with near-light speed through space, only to reunite the split substances back into the whole … I was reborn a different man, changed irreversibly into a new being.

I was in love.

"Hi!" I said.

Her hair, a rampage of burnt orange, reeled around her face like rivulets, drenching her shoulders and radiating a glow around her. I'd never seen such hair before, or since. Her skin was smooth and porcelain-like. I yearned to touch it.

"Great party, right?"

She kept silent, standing remarkably still next to the piano. Her breath, quick and shallow, drifted in and out through half-opened lips. Her chest rising and falling, the frills of her lilac dress quivering.

"Won't you sing some more?" I pleaded and stepped forward.

She gasped and backed away, hitting the wall behind her. An alarm rang somewhere in my head. What did I do? Why is she so scared?

Her friend Eva came and 'borrowed' her 'for a sec', and she ran.

I pursued her relentlessly for weeks, organising parties and inviting her, bribing her girlfriends to lure her out of the house, settling on the street she lived on for most mornings and afternoons with a big crowd of my supporters. We would compose some loud commotion to attract her attention. The neighbourhood bore it with curiosity and anticipation for a happy union, at first. As weeks past, they shooed us away complaining of the noise.

I persisted; the neighbours sent 'the elder' to explain that she was not interested. After a few days, she moved in with her parents and sisters and in a few more months, she married another man.

That's when my endless strolls across the city started. Like a walking wounded, I sought for something that would make me whole again. I'd wake at dawn and wander the streets for hours, literally debating and arguing with her in my head ... trying to persuade her that I was the only right choice. There were times I would declare my love to her and tell endless tales of our future life together. There were times I would blame her with bitter hatred for being so blind. Her voice in my head would wake me up in the nights, my chest hurting, starved of oxygen and struggling for breath, tears flowing and choking me.

Then the day arrived when I realised that I couldn't blame her anymore, for she had made her choice she was free to make. How could you blame someone for loving another?

I buried my heart that day and busied myself with work and study. In eight months, I graduated and shortly moved away, drifting from place to place, unable to stop and settle down, only to return in two decades.

I follow the Metekhi Street down to the deserted riverbank. The grey of the day dyes the surroundings with blues. Through the drabness of the place, I see a lonely figure in the distance – a vaguely familiar figure. I stare at her standing on the promenade remarkably still, watching the river. Her hair of burnt orange beats in the cold wind like the thick waters below. I freeze on the pavement. That color ... those rebellious curls ... can it possibly be her? The fireworks within me confirm the impossible. She's there, just a few minutes of walking distance from me. A soft, almost undetectable gasp escapes my lips.

"Anaid …"

III Davit and Anaid

A flock of swallows flits across the sky, their chirping tinkles in the air.

He watches her climbing up onto the parapet, each move awkward and uncertain. A gust of wind catches her hair baring the lines of her neck and shoulders.

He can hear the river below calling her, he can sense the powerful pull she's unable to resist much longer. A feeling of terror and dread of what is about to happen settles in his heart and accelerates its beat.

The increased blood supply allows his nerve cells to talk faster to each other and pace up the release of neurotransmitters. A hundred billion neurons in his brain work swiftly seeking solution.

Through the despairing agony he wills for time to halt, to save the woman he loves.

Thoughts that pass through his head are chaotic and not linked to each other. He curses Newton's belief that time travels like an arrow, he praises Einstein's statement that time is like a meandering river, speeding up and slowing down.

The involuntary decision to run begins and travels through numerous structures of his nervous system before reaching the muscles of his legs.

All that happens essentially in half the time of a blink of an eye.

Shoulders back, his body leaning low to the ground, he propels himself forward. Arms swinging, taking long powerful strides, he runs like never before.

Each step is hard and takes an incredible effort to make, for he moves against the time that exists in his reality. He shouts instructions to his limbs to move faster, "Run! Run! Run!" And watches the time falling behind, whilst he speeds up.

She's still on the parapet, arms stretched out, motionless. Her hair is suspended in the air in a stationary chaos. The flock of birds hangs static in the sky, their shadows lay still on the lifeless river below. Their cry is cancelled, yet the air still holds an indiscernible droning and quivering of their call, amassed into a singularity of some sort.

Am I hallucinating? Is it just my feverish mind creating an illusion? Is she still there? Yes!

Here the time stands still, decelerated into a merely passive inert entity.

Love for her pumps and beats and surges through his system and erupts like molten rocks, reaching for her.

He can still stop her, stop the irreversible, however imperceptible the time span he has left to reach her – he can save her. There is a possibility of the impossible. And that possibility is right here right now, granted to him.

Facing ahead, eyes on the woman he loves, he runs for the impossible. He sees nothing, but the lonely figure standing on the parapet. "Faster! Faster! Faster!"

Each step feels like a birth of truth.

JULIE RYAN

My roots are in a small mining village in South Yorkshire. After a degree in French Language and Literature, wanderlust kicked in and I have lived and worked in France, Poland, Thailand and Greece. Using the latter as inspiration I started a series of mystery romances/ thrillers set in the Greek Isles.

Jenna's Journey is the first novel in the Series, a series I did not set out to create but which took on its own life and grew, highlighting the hidden dark sides of dream vacations in the Greek Isles. Pandora's Prophecy and Sophia's Secret make up the rest of the trilogy. After self-publishing the trilogy, the first book was taken up by publishers Booktrope until they ceased operations.

Determined to take my writing seriously I enrolled in 2019 as part of the first cohort of Hull University's Masters in Creative Writing and am thrilled to have successfully completed the course- one of the best things I've ever done..

A prolific and well-known book review blogger, I do my writing and reviewing from rural Gloucestershire, where I live with my husband, son and dippy cat with half a tail.

A GLOUCESTERSHIRE GHOST STORY

'Looks can be deceptive.' There was but the slightest hint of a warning in the landlord's tone as he took a puff of his pipe before he continued, 'We who know her are familiar with her moods. Calm and tranquil one day, a raging monster the next. A seductive siren with a tinkling laugh, or a heinous harpy, clutching you in her claws?'

I thought he was talking about one of the customers, but a quick glance around the inn told me that, except for myself, it was empty.

'The Severn. The most beautiful yet treacherous river in England.'

His words still ringing in my ears, I set off towards the river undeterred. It was the first really warm, spring day of the year and far too pleasant to let the curmudgeonly landlord dampen my mood.

Built by the Romans, my guidebook informed me, the road runs straight for almost a mile until you reach the river. I walked at a steady pace, calculating that I should arrive in less than thirty minutes, and should have worked up a fine appetite for lunch on my return.

It was a picture perfect rural scene, the air redolent with rebirth, the trees in bud alive with birdsong, fields fecund with crops. As if to add the final layer to this Gloucestershire idyll, a lamb just a few weeks old, poked its head through a fence, baaing in contentment. I stood spellbound admiring the skill of a spider furiously spinning her web until once finished, she lay in wait, lurking patiently for her prey.

I was so engrossed in the tranquillity of this scene that I didn't immediately notice the woman on the path ahead. I had no idea how long she'd been standing there.

At first I thought she must be a mirage. The sun was directly in my eyes so I rubbed them but when I looked again, she was still there. Only then did I notice her hair, hanging in braids around her face, droplets of water glinting in the sunlight. She held out her hand, beckoning me to join her. I longed to run my fingers through those silken tresses, to entwine my fingers in hers. I stood transfixed.

"Move closer,' she whispered, 'don't be shy. Closer now.'

Her voice was so soft and beguiling that a man could drown in her words; the soft sibilant tone as hypnotic as the snake charmer's melody.

I couldn't help noticing how her diaphanous dress clung to her form revealing lithe limbs beneath. I tried to avert my gaze, of course, but found myself following the droplets of water that trickled down a delicate pale throat, before pooling between her breasts. A gentle ripple coursed through my veins. I had no choice but to follow her as she beckoned me towards pools of water sparkling in the sun at the river's edge.

The tide was on the turn, the river a silvery streak, the silted riverbed the same colour as the earthen banks, the stench of mud oozing from the silt; squelching, stinking mud that sucked you in; hard to know where the mud bank ended and the river began.

I felt myself being pulled in, deeper and deeper until, eddying and swirling, the incoming current took me towards her. Sound muffled. The birds stopped singing, the only song that of the river.

It was only much later, seated by a roaring fire in the inn that I realised what a lucky escape I'd had. Were it not for the innkeeper following me in his horse and cart and pulling me from the river, I wouldn't be here to tell the tale.

I thanked the man for his kindness in saving my life and asked him if he knew the identity of the woman I'd seen. His reply chilled me.

'Did you look upon her face?' he asked.

I nodded.

'Not such a lucky escape then. Once you have looked upon the face of Sabrina, a death is imminent.'

At the time, I didn't fully comprehend his meaning. I had to wait another year for the full import of his words to come true. But it is late now so that is a story for another day.

THE TRIALS OF HARRY BURTON

(Written tapescript of responses to investigator's questions)

1. Janice Mary Burton
2. 43
3. Born and bred in God's own county, Yorkshire
4. Sorry, 28 Station Road, Barnsley, South Yorkshire
5. Just meself and me twin sons, Harry and Iain. Well, I say twins but they've got different dads. I 'ant seen Harry's dad since he were born. Bit of a wheeler-dealer type. Got me knocked up and then did a disappearin' act. Right Houdini he were. That's why I called me boy 'Arry.
6. It' s a bit complicated and I'm not sure I reight understand but they do say it's possible if the woman has sex with two people in a short time. That's why they're not identical. I know what you're thinking but it weren't like that. I mean, Harry's dad got me drunk on pina coladas and took advantage.
7. 17. They're both seventeen.
8. When he was a baby. Harry's allus been fearless. I remember when the twins were just toddlers and we went for a picnic in t'woods near our house. They both goes off for a wander like and Harry comes back holding a snake. Well, I nearly had 'eart attack I can tell

you. In the end it turns out it were only a grass snake but Harry didn't know that. He killed it reight in front of his brother who was screaming his 'ead off.

9. No.

10. You can't count that. He only got a caution. Besides, he meant no harm. He's allus been fascinated by animals. Anyhow he were only twelve then and the zoo didn't press charges once they got all the deer back. Well, except for the one that the wild boar killed.

11. That lion died of natural causes.

12. Coincidence

13. Look, my lad were trying to make amends for letting the deer out. He spent every weekend cleaning out the big cat shelter. Have you ever smelt lion shit? Well it stinks. Bad. Even after he'd had a shower and changed his clothes the stench was still there. Ended up hosing him down in the yard. There were bits of lion shit stuck to the pebbledash for months.

14. That was Iain's idea.

15. Iain's the techie one. Well. It were during the summer holidays and Mr Weaver who has the farm near my cousin was complaining about the birds eating all his crops. Seems the scarecrow idea hadn't worked. Iain checked out YouTube and found a clip with a WW2 siren. He's dead clever is my Iain. Rigged it up to an old speaker he did. Got rid of the birds a treat. The farmer was well pleased.

16. That was unfortunate.

17. How was he to know it would go off accidentally at 3am and scare Mrs Wilson half to death?

18. Like I said, it was unfortunate but as far as I know she did make a full recovery. Eventually.

19. Of course I did.

20. Both of them went and helped the farmer with milking the cows for a week. Thought it would keep them out of trouble an' all.

21. No.

22. Well, it's all done by electric machines now, so, when the cows had been milked, the boys had to lead them back to the field.

23. Not exactly.

24. Harry was in front and Iain at the rear to keep the cows together. Then Harry's mobile rang. Apparently, he shot off down one of the lanes to see if he could get a better reception and all the cows followed him. You can just picture it, can't you? My Harry leading these cows down the lane only it's a dead end. They have no idea how to turn a herd of cows round. It was amazin'. Harry put the photos on Instagram later.

25. About three hours. Nobody could get in or out. The farmer wasn't best pleased. Still, no damage done, eh?

26. That was different.

27. It would never have happened if the farmer hadn't let the bull out at that exact moment.

28. Have you ever seen a bull close up? They're huge and if it fancies a bit of 'howsyerfather'

there's no stopping it. Harry was very brave waiting until it had finished before leading it back.

29. Well, after that I did ground him for two weeks. Trouble is, two boys under yer feet gets to yer after a while, so when Josie – that's the barmaid in the pub where I do the cleaning on Mondays and Wednesdays, said her sister runs a horse-riding stables and the boys could have half-price riding lessons in return for mucking out, well I jumped at the chance.

30. No.

31. Well, he fancies himself as a cowboy so one day, he dresses up in his Stetson and tries to lasso one of the horses. Iain took a brilliant photo on his iPhone – and before you ask, it ain't knocked off. Iain's dad bought it for hi birthday. Put Harry's nose out a bit, I can tell yer. Harry's dad never even sends him a birthday card. Anyway, Josie's sister isn't too happy and now Josie isn't speaking to me. Still, it don't matter. I've got a new job as a cleaner in a lab. Better hours and better money so it's a win-win really.

32. We've put that behind us. He's doing okay at school now. He's really quite bright. Must take after me.

33. I agree. Breaking into his teacher's house was totally unacceptable.

34. But he gave it back to her the next day so you can't really charge him with stealing anything.

35. Okay I'll give you breaking and entering but he's a kid for heaven's sake. High spirits. Anyway he apologised and spent two days in isolation at school.

36. You can't pin that on him. He never threatened her and if she chose to leave the school, well that's her decision. I still think she shouldn't have reported it. I mean, it were only a belt. If he'd wanted to nick something, he'd have chosen something more valuable. She never liked him. Pity, 'cos until this happened I think Harry had a soft spot for her. He was allus going on about 'Miss Briggs this and Miss Briggs that.' He never thought she'd take is so serious. Science is his favourite subject.

37. No, in hindsight he shouldn't have posted pictures of her belt on Facebook.

38. Oh, I wondered when you'd get to that.

39. Look, I've done me best to bring my boys up proper. Have you got kids? If you have, you'll know that boys can he a handful but my two know right from wrong. Those boys want for nothing. As soon as I've got a bit saved up, I'll buy Harry his own iPhone then he won't have to borrow his brother's.

40. How was I to know they was solid gold?

41. You can't do that. There's no way I would have 'ad them apples in my house if I'd known. No way am I an accomplice.

42. Allright, so he took 'em without permission but it's some stupid challenge on *Howfarwillyougo*.

43. So, technically it is theft but he planned to return them. They said it couldn't be done but I told you Harry's clever, didn't I? Something to do with a skylight and magnets. I think that boy has been watching too much James Bond. Iain helped with the burglar alarm. Reckon he's got a great future in electronics. Anyway when I saw the golden apples in Harry's bedroom, I thought he'd gone all arty. I mean, there's no way you think they're real gold, right? Must be worth a fortune.

44. How much?

45. Let me speak to him. I'm sure we can sort this out. Like I said, these pranks are all part of an online challenge. Luckily, he's through to the final and there's only one more challenge left. He won't tell me what it is though. I know there's a huge prize for the winner, so who knows, he might make his fortune like one of them You Tube stars. He's already got quite a following or so he tells me.

46. Look, I promise to take responsibility for him. In fact, he's knuckling down for his science 'A' levels. Suddenly developed an interest in genetics and cloning, would you believe? Keeps asking if I can get him a job in the lab. That would be great. I could keep an eye on him there. I mean, what mischief could he get up to?

47. Oh that's brilliant. I knew you were a good 'un. It'll make all the difference not having this on his record.

48. I will. Might get him a dog. He's been asking for one and it would keep him fit. What do you reckon?

I declare this is a true version of events.

…………………………………………………………………..
signed   date

DAMION SPENCER

Damion Spencer is a Jamaican living in Japan. He has a B.Ed. in Literacy Studies from the University of the West Indies, Mona, a PGCert in Psychology from the University of Liverpool and an MA in Creative Writing from the University of Hull. His short story 'Bunka Bat and Sour Orange' was recently published in Volume No.35 of The Caribbean Writer, a spectacular tribute edition celebrating literary giant Kamau Brathwaite. Damion was also shortlisted for the 2021 Queen Mary Wasafiri New Writing Prize in the Life Writing category.

He is currently working on his debut memoir, Unmasking the Spirits, a life-affirming portrait, exploring the complexities of male alexithymia. He enjoys writing on train commutes around Tokyo, rewatching old movies and obsessing over game shows and puzzles. He and his wife share a home with their two wonderful children—a moody teenager and a needy toddler.

Naseberry Season

I live in Cascade with my mother and father. Just us three in a big white house on a hill. I have fun days licking baking tins, getting piggyback rides, and stringing needles and replacing bobbin threads. My mother is about fifty different people in one and I love all of them.

She changes her colour like a croaking lizard. And I'm not talking about the spreading white spots on her face that she daubs in nutmeg pressed powder before climbing onto our verandah each morning, which hangs above the main road like a naseberry branch with more fruits than leaves. Come to think of it, our house is like a feeding tree perching on a hillside, where both hungry people and animals from all over the community visit daily. "Call me aunty," she tells everybody. I sure call her aunty, too. She wears many hats in the community. With a thimble and thread, she is magic, she has the greenest thumb—a talent that makes her President of the local Horticulture Society. Aunty is also Women's Fellowship Leader and Choir Director at church, maybe because she is the pastor's wife.

But it's the little battles we fight around the yard, I remember best. She's the army general and I'm the foot soldier. We set up a beachhead against sooty mold on her prized Parson Brown orange tree. Mealybugs, aphids and whiteflies are our fiercest enemies. A few chicken hawks and egg-thieving dogs are seasonal mercenaries that suffer at the arsenal of her left hand. She never misses. And some days we both sit on the verandah steps nursing the wasp bites we get from clearing the nests hanging under the eaves of the roof.

Sometimes, before day breaks, we are up, two curtain-twitchers lying in wait for the neighbour and his goats as they come running down the hill. We have to be out in front of the house standing guard over the line of crotons. Broom in hand and threatening to put a whooping in the goat man's pants seat if his goats ever touch the flowers. Whatever plants the goats nibble, struggle and eventually die. I guess this is where the 'goat mouth' saying comes from. If someone says you have goat mouth, it means that your mouth spoils people's business or simply put, stops progress.

Ms. Whitaker, my Sunday school teacher has goat mouth. "Sister Parry, Kevin is not behaving," she screeches in her plummy voice, spoiling a good game of cowplop bingo. Having the children's lesson on the outside and close to the cow pasture, is a recipe for disaster. All that open space sends the imagination galloping all over the place. So, I have my bible studies with the adult class inside the church on those tough cedar benches, reading all the scriptures—thanks to Ms. Whitaker. She teaches at my primary school as well. Like the Sankey says, anywhere the army go Satan follow. Her penmanship and elocution lessons are no joke. It is like fighting for Queen and country. I like her though. She makes the best egg flips on Christmas Day.

Pastor Parry is more laidback than aunty. He is not at home much. I guess making new churches and baptizing new saints keep him busy. Oh, he works on his farm too. He's a big farmer. Not the hoe and cutlass farmer. He has tractors and his produce don't go to the market. Pastor Parry is in the export business and selling to the hotels in Ocho Rios. I sometimes go with him when he makes deliveries at the hotels. Ocho Rios is nice. I eat the best ice-creams there. Not like the soupy-soupy kinds Creamy sells from his bike as he rides up and down in the sun, honking his horn. I go to extra lesson in Ocho Rios at my teacher's house. I don't remember the name of the place, but Pastor Parry and I walk pass a pink house every time I go to class, where there are some women who smile and wave as if they know him. There are many big stones in front of the pink house. Maybe they are too heavy for the women to move. Pastor Parry can help them. He is a strong farmer, but he hurries me along and tells me not to look at the women. I get to see the ocean on our walk to teacher's house.

"The babbling brooks and wild rivers end up here, eight of them to be exact," Pastor Parry tells me. He loves history. That's how I learn that Ocho Rios is Spanish for eight rivers.

My favourite of the eight, is the Dunn's River Falls. I also like the White River since it's where I learn to swim and where Pastor Parry holds his baptisms. He stands out in the middle of a blue hole, where the water is chest high. The congregation stands on both sides of the river singing happy hymns as the baptismal candidates stream into the river in white gowns like foam when a river comes down bank-to-bank and no blue is in sight. The singing stops. They listen to the vows and repeat them. White gown disappears under the water and reappears to the joyous tune of, we shall have a new name in that land...

The best part of the baptism is always the altar call. Pastor Parry spreads his arms and begs the onlookers,

"Turn from your wicked ways and come to Christ." One time this drunk, full of shame, staggers forward from the crowd. And just like that, a tears and snot-swaddled face stumbles towards the deep end. Baptism quickly turns to a rescue mission as the man begins to swallow more water than the liquor he is drinking. His vows are more an oath against God than a promise to be a servant. The good pastor makes a dash for him and drags him to safety on dry land. The little excitement becomes an object lesson, "Christ leaves the ninety and nine and goes in search of the one lost sheep," Pastor Parry tells the crowd and then adds a little joke that this particular man would have gone down a dry sinner and came up a wet one seeing how he curses and howl like a storm when water touches his skin.

Storms are no joke. It is a big storm that break down the giant naseberry tree, falling it and showing the roots like God himself pull it out from its place and put it elsewhere. No flowers, no farm, nobody goes outside. Tin food is our saviour. At least when we have the Bully beef key. If not, we rub the can on the wall until it open. I sleep with the clothes on my bed like a fortress. They keep me warm. Aunty tells me not to get off the bed because if I catch whooping cough, I have to drink rat soup. I don't even eat Bully beef, so I am not chancing rat soup.

Things start to change after the storm. First, Ms. Whitaker leaves for England, taking her egg flip recipe with her. I see less of Pastor Parry. "What breeze blow you here?" Aunty asks when he does show up for us to go to Ocho Rios. Everything look new in Ocho Rios, the roads, the buildings, even the ocean – when I get to see it.

But was this all true? I couldn't say. Remembering my childhood was always like walking through smog from burning green grass. Like looking out for Aunty at the end of her nightly prayer meetings as she walked up the path wearing her favourite grey velvet dress and the broadest church hat.

The things that spell my childhood were fast disappearing.

**

In 1988 four Jamaican army boys and a supporter warmed the hearts of the world at the Winter Olympics held in Calgary despite crashing their bobsled; hurricane Gilbert barrelled across the island leaving no stones unturned; and the Los Angeles Dodgers snatched the world series from the Oakland Athletics.

The hurricane pummelled Jamaica pretty much like what the Dodgers had done to the team from the West Coast but as fate would have it, from this loss came great fortune for some at least, as championship shirts turned up in poor-relief barrels shipped to the island. I wore my Athletics shirt like a true fan. It was a year of little giving and great taking. I had no choice but to take what I could.

A whirlwind myself, I blew into the lives of the Parry's. Good folks. They turned out to be fertile soil for me, a seedling uprooted from its hatching bed. I was nurtured, loved, spoiled even like a wash belly should but vague memories visited me, damped my young soul – thoughts formed like dew each night in my bed. For years I had strange dreams of being washed down a wild river and a scythe biting at my heels in a patch of tall grass. Drowning. Sometimes in tears and sweat. Other times I awoke from these nightmares, rank and soaked in piss. Only the memories, formed in Ocho Rios gave better dreams for my nights.

In preparation for the Common Entrance Exams in primary school, I took extra classes at my teacher's house in Old Buckfield—a quaint residential community that sat on a bluff, overlooking the beautiful Caribbean Sea.

I would get off the taxi in Pineapple and walk across a ghetto to get to her house. During this time, the grand highway was being built. It would connect Coconut Grove, across from the Irie FM radio station with the intersection at Evelyn Street downtown. This way you could avoid the bumper-to-bumper traffic, the maddening market that spilled onto the streets, and the handful of tourists lost in an ocean of local sellers. The only trouble was, the highway was slated to run straight through Pink House—a house of naked women.

"Hold your head straight," Pastor Parry would say, hauling me behind him through the boulders and ditches.

"Who are…"

"Heathens!" He would tell me before the question left my lips.

I learned not to ask but it didn't stop me from peeking through the corner of my eyes. The ladies always seemed happy to see Pastor Parry but before the end of summer, the Pink House was gone. From my teacher's house, I could see the rust-covered metal roof at Reynold's Pier. The ochre patina stained on the lazy blue sky was the definition of a Caribbean sunset. Growing hotels and shopping malls promised that this view will soon be gone.

Later as a young adult, I learned that the women of pink house were prostitutes. And just as the sleepy fishing village of Ocho Rios was waking up to a new world, these women were about to paint the entire town pink. If selling tail was a vehicle, the smiles and miniskirt worn by the displaced women of Pink House, were premium gas.

Prostitution took off at bird speed and men from all around the world flocked to Ocho Rios. Sadly, even men like Pastor Parry. He spent so many years preaching against the vices of vile men, only to succumb to the very evil. It was around this time I found out that the Parry's weren't my biological parents. Coupled with the merciless jeering at school and the one teacher who took an interest in me moving back to England, I was in limbo. I did not know who I was and every effort to find answers, got stuck in whatever the Parry's were experiencing.

I remembered them arguing about me going to visit my mother. It started in the dining room and poured into the kitchen. Aunty paced across the kitchen floor, picking up and dropping every little thing in sight. She paused at the sink, gripped the counter with both hands and buried her head between her shoulders.

She sucked her teeth before speaking. "I knew this day would come."

"What troubles you dear," Pastor Parry inquired, closing his bible, and resting it on the dining table.

"Can you be so blind?"

"It's just for a few weeks."

"Yes, and then it's Christmas, and before you know it, we'll be the ones begging to see him."

"Calm down."

"Don't tell me to calm," Aunty smashed a dinner plate, cutting her hand.

"My love please don't be angry, look what you did."

"These hands, fed him, bathe him, nursed him for years and now they're as good as being chopped off."

"Gloria, that's enough," said Pastor Parry, grabbing her wounded hand.

"Just leave me alone. You're on their side."

"There's no side to this, love."

"There's no me, that's what this is."

"How can you say that?"

"How can I not?"

"Kevin has a right to know his folks."

"We are his folks! Well, me at least as you are clearly out of the picture"

"Let's not do this in front of the boy."

"I'd never thought that I'd raised such an unthankful, ungrateful…"

"Gloria."

"…Serpent tooth, spiteful boy…"

"Gloria!"

"What?"

"Enough!"

"What about me?"

"You will always have Kevin, dear. He's our son too."

"Am I not a woman?"

"Of course, dear."

"Some women can handpick when they want to be a mother."

"Gloria don't trouble yourself."

"Let me trouble myself!"

"The boy will spend some time with them and be home to you, his mother."

"You can say anything! If he goes, I'll be alone."

"Don't say that."

"What, you don't think he knows what you're doing in Ocho Rios?"

"There you go…"

"Maybe he should go after all."

"No, I'll go."

"There must be a man with a backbone to teach him how to be a real man out there."

Pastor Parry did not reply. He only walked out of the kitchen that evening and straight out of our lives. The best man I knew got up and left me at the mercy of all these women. I spent the rest of primary school walking in a triangle. Home, school, and church. I had only women to teach me how to be a man at this point and boy did they hate men. Aunty's advice was mostly not to be like Pastor Parry, my teachers on the other hand had mantras like 'reading maketh the man', 'teach a man to fish and you feed him for life', and for a long while I thought men were to be reading fishermen. But it was the Women's Fellowship at church that waged the biggest war on men. They had service outside of the bars and warned us not to drink or we would become worthless men. They would visit the men's prisons, hospitals, and infirmaries to scare us boys from a life of violence and frivolity. This only gave me more nightmares. I wanted to believe that a man took care of his family by feeding and providing for them. Maybe a man is a father who took his children out for ice-cream or walk with them to school. Pastor Parry did all these things but now maybe he's not so much of a man since he no longer does these things for his family. Who knows? Besides, Aunty was never going to be outdone by a man.

She asked me to do the dishes one day and I told her how one of my classmates said it was a woman's job to do the dishes. Aunty smiled.

"But it's a man's job."

"Really? Then again, there's no way to prove it."

"I will wipe Jerusalem as a man wipeth a dish, wiping it, and turning it upside down"

"That's in the bible?"

"2 Kings 21:13, God's words," she said, handing me the big family bible.

She had quickly replaced Pastor Parry with God himself. Aunty promised me that we were going to be ok, but her vitiligo had spread further on her face and little by little she crumbled under the shame of the pastor and stopped going out. She was a recluse – a wraithlike figure hiding in the house. Auntie would take on sewing jobs to cover our bills but fashion was not big in the conservative church and so our light got cut off first and then the water. Luckily for us they left the pipe in the yard so at nights we would fill our vessels. With no electricity, we had to use kerosene oil lamps and a coal iron. Smelling like woodfire did not help with the teasing at school, but I didn't care much at this point. Aunty was being both man and woman at home, teaching me to be a resilient person instead of just a mere man.

It was just Aunty and me. No church friends. Nobody. We couldn't afford shopping at the supermarket, so we planted our own food. On special days like my birthday, she would have me catch a common fowl from the yard a week before, gave it cane vinegar to cleanse it and have it prepared. As much as I welcomed the meat, skipping the deluge of vegetables we consumed, killing, and eating common fowl was risky business. She would stretch the neck of the fowl under an enamel bath pan, sat on it until the weight chopped the head clean off the fowl. It then flatters under the pan until all the life bled out. Then we dipped the headless fowl in a pot of boiling water for a few seconds, picked the feathers and plucked the guts.

This was the time I didn't missed the electricity because without a refrigerator we had to eat the fowl as quickly as possible. Two days tops, three if we smoked it over the fireplace. After all that work, you best be careful when eating this kind of meat. A common fowl bone can shatter like glass and wound you in the mouth.

In the whirlwind of fiery darts hurled from the pot mouth of my peers, came some good news. Exam results were out, and I was going to high school. I was leaving most of who called me "fatherless" and teased me about wearing a blouse to school—well that was true. Aunty made my shirt like a blouse. She was happy that something good had happened for us, but she was just as concerned. High school meant money. We even forgot how money had looked by then. I could still wear my old uniform because it was the same khaki fabric for high school but as for my shoes, it would have been better to walk barefooted. If I close my eyes and the cardboard wore out, I could tell you where I was in Cascade just by how the gravels and stones felt.

While we were there contemplating the difficulties ahead, two big parcels stamped with Royal mail insignia came for us. We weren't entirely out of friends. A fresh pair of brown suede British Knights, school supplies, several suits of Seaman khaki, and a leather rucksack for me. Aunty got her own things. I was all set for high school, but this was where things took a turn for the worse

WASH BELLY

Darkness descended in strands about the place like a young maiden's raven-black tresses tumbling from under her bonnet after offloading a bankra basket stacked with beefy, blacky and number eleven.

I walked with Papa Thompson in measured strides, sizing him up, looking for some resemblance. Not much could be seen in the ribbon of darkness that webbed between the hibiscus fences, whose blossoms were already gathering the tears of the evening. The night dew cooled our weary feet. Papa Thompson whistled through the darkness and a female voice answered like a cooing pigeon.

"We de nearing home," he said. We came upon a humble cottage, in a little clearing, nestled between what appeared to be banana and cocoa trees. And just in front of the outdoor kitchen stood a fair-skinned woman holding out a lantern to light our path. When I came face-to-face with the woman, and saw who she was, a series of involuntary memories stirred and buzzed in my brain like a swarm of bees darting across a pasture of marigold.

"Eheh, a can't believe mi eyes," said Ms. Kate.

"You remembered me, mama," I searched her face for her reaction.

"Memba you? I carried you in ma bosom every single day that Massa God send." "Aye, mek wi come out the night dew and go inside," said Papa Thompson.

"Get away from me, I waited many moons for dis day," said Ms. Kate, as she latched on to my neck.

Her tears burned my skin as they trickled down. Her thick calico dress pickled in smoke and the dinner of boiled food and shad smelt like the country—smelt like home.

Ms. Kate wept. Not a stylish sob. She wailed as in the dirge at the end of a ring shout, when the chant is riddled in pain like a young woman forced to name the throes, that must be endured to have her womb emptied-out of her first child.

I kept flooding my lungs with the crisp night air. My tongue stabbed to the roof of my mouth like Jacob's ladder up to heaven. I tried everything not to shed a tear. But over Ms Kate's shoulder, a creeper plant, toiled, toiled upward until it was sat on the old kitchen's windowsill. Swelled. Then spilled off in silver streams as moonlight dripped from each tendril.

And just as how dew gathered on a coco leaf will at some point be too heavy to hold, every tear finally fell out of me.

"Yo not a Water Mada a church fi notn," chided Papa Thompson.

"Lawks, puss bruck coconut ina yo face mek you no cry?" Ms. Kate answered, pulling off her head tie and sapping her face dry.

"Yo come," she said to me, "Yo jes in time fi some bikl."

She transferred from the hug to a one-handed hold, like how one prod a recalcitrant child against his will. This was how I was marched into the kitchen. She hauled down a calabash from the creng creng mesh, hung over the fireplace, smoking meat. She brushed it clean with her frock tail and packed in the food.

"Yo not s'pose to be picky wid food, Yo almost skin and bones," Ms. Kate mumbled as she tossed another chunk of yellow yam into the calabash.

"He lucky to find pot on fire during mango season," Papa Thompson said chuckling. "Zackly," Ms. Kate agreed, then added, "jes a stone throw behind the kitchen is a loaded blacky mango tree."

"Woman Kiba yo mouth," barked Papa Thompson "He boun to find out!"

Ms. Kate stormed out of the kitchen. I didn't speak. The convivial atmosphere plunged into dead silence. Then the wind came whispering thorough the wooden slabs. Blackened by woodfire, they were night's lips calling my attention to Papa Thompson sat across from me, stone-faced like a grave with a bitter secret.

ANNA MIRFIN

Anna Mirfin has completed an MA in Creative Writing and is now working on her first book A Family in Mind, which examines generational trauma through the lives of her own family. She is a primary school teacher and mother of two who began writing as a form of therapy and now writes fearlessly whenever she has the opportunity. Writing has both saved and inspired her.

GRANTING SERENITY

Holding his cloth satchel adorned with badges calling on us to "Save the Bees" and to "Free Tibet", Andy walked up his garden path towards the back door of his bungalow. The late summer sun cast long shadows before him and the scent of neatly tended roses was thick in the humid air. Bees thrummed aggressively around the lavender, a sure sign of a looming storm, and a neighbourhood cat padded softly past.

The garden was well-tended although a tangle of wild flowers had been allowed a measure of freedom and a large buddleia sprawled next to a newly painted shed which Andy used for meditation and in which the occasional spider made its home. Colourful flags had been strung across the garden and fluttered brightly whenever there was a breeze, little prayers being whispered for the good of mankind.

Before he went inside, he checked the bird feeder and, finding it empty, shook his head in amusement, scanning the sky for his feathery friends.

He removed his shoes and walked into the kitchen, placing his bag on the scrubbed wooden table where he and June ate. The room sparkled and Andy thought, not for the first time, how lucky he had been in meeting June and what she had ever seen in him God only knew. He pulled off his lucky baseball cap which had been his only attempt at recapturing his youth, eased on his slippers and walked into the bathroom. Inside framed quotations littered the walls instructing the observer to "Walk a mile in my shoes", or observe the teachings of the Dalai Lama and "Be kind whenever possible. It is always possible."

After washing his hands, he made himself a coffee and was about to go into the garden when the phone rang.

'Hello.' A pause. Only a faint sound of breathing told him that someone was there. 'Hello, can you hear me?' he tried, glancing at his phone to ensure the volume was up.

'Is that Andy… Andy Tann?'

'Yes, it is, but I don't want to buy anything thank you.'

'No…oh God this is difficult; I'm Nate, your grandson.'

Andy held the phone tightly, his fingers reddening from the pressure. 'Nate,' he breathed trying to comprehend what was happening but failing completely. 'Nate, my Nate?'

'I think so; my mum was Helen, Helen Tann.'

'Was?' Andy looked wildly around him needing June's serenity but she wasn't there.

'That's why I'm calling… mum died yesterday morning; she had cancer and…' He halted, trying unsuccessfully to choke back a sob. 'I'm sorry to have to tell you Andy, but Mum asked me to; she wrote me a letter for after she'd…' Another pause. '…well for after. And she told me to invite you to the funeral and to tell you that she…she loved you.'

Andy tried to speak but nothing would come. Tears streamed in silent rivers along the crags of his face, staining his trousers unforgivingly. He thought of a drink, but it was fleeting - an old response to pain. A rumble of thunder rolled across the sky and rain began to course down the panes.

After a moment he heard a voice calling. 'Andy…Andy?'

'Sorry Nate, yes I'm here. It's just all a bit much, you know.'

'Yeah, I do.'

'I…I loved her very much.'

'I know Andy; she told me that and, well, it would have meant a lot to her if you would come to the funeral. It would mean a lot to me too.'

'It would be an honour Nate,' he replied.

They talked for a few minutes longer, neither wanting to end the conversation but not knowing what else to say. Andy arranged to meet Nate on the day of the funeral and assured him that he was happy to have heard from him despite the circumstances.

'Well, goodbye Nate and thank you; I know how difficult this call must have been for you, but I'm…I'm glad you made it.'

'So am I Andy. Mum always knew best.'

Later, after June had come home and they had cried together, he went back into the garden. It was damp from the rain, which had cleansed the sky, and a fresh more hopeful breeze blew.

He refilled the bird feeder and sat down on a chair from the kitchen. He pulled out a picture of his daughter from his wallet and finding a particular recording he had made on his mobile, pressed play. The sweet sound of birdsong burst through the speakers as he imagined her soaring with abandon across the night sky.

PHYSICIAN HEAL THYSELF

Standing stiffly by the window, Adam sighed. He'd known they would come, but he wasn't ready. Could he ever have been? A cane struck the door forcibly and Adam opened it, swinging it wide.

'Ah Adam, I am Councillor Andrews and this is Mr Thomas; we are here on behalf of the city,' said a softly spoken older man stepping into the dimly lit interior, fingers careful not to touch anything. He was followed closely, by a smaller bewhiskered man carrying a large leather bag and smelling of vinegar.

Sitting, both men considered Adam who stood uncertainly by the table and the remnants of his supper.

'Please sit down,' the bewhiskered man smiled, gesturing to a stool.

'Oh, I prefer to stand if it's all the same to you, Sir.'

'Please,' he repeated keeping his careful smile in place.

Lowering himself into a chair on the opposite side of the table, Adam splayed his fingers over the rough wooden table seeking reassurance from its bulk. Looking down he examined his hands and noticing his black finger nails, he covered them blushing.

'Adam, I am sure you know why we are here,' said Councillor Andrews waiting until Adam lifted his head and made eye contact. 'Since the tragic death of your employer, we are of course now in need of another doctor for this part of the city and as his apprentice, this most important of jobs has befallen to you. We have come here tonight to provide you with the necessary…tools for your position.' Bending, he lifted the leather bag onto the table.

Adam stared at it trembling.

'Sirs, I was only at the start of my apprenticeship when the good Doctor was struck down. I have not the knowledge or the skills to take his place. What good can I do?'

Councillor Andrews leant backwards in his chair saying nothing, seemingly lost in thought. After a moment, he focused his intelligent eyes on Adam's and gently questioned, 'Do you believe in God?'

'I do Sir.'

'And you have faith in His power and love?'

'I do.'

'Then you have nothing to fear young Adam. God will protect you.' Councillor Andrews pulled a Bible from the leather bag and pushed it across the table. He unblinkingly held Adam's stare until looking down, the young man drew the book towards him.

'We need you Adam, the people of London need you. Will you forsake them? Can you forsake them?'

The smell of vinegar assaulted Adam's nostrils as the bewhiskered man approached and pressed a string of amber beads attached to a silver cross into his hands. Then, opening the bag, he brought out the mask and laid it almost reverentially, so that its curved beak pointed towards Adam.

After the men had left, with only the faint aroma of vinegar lingering in the air, Adam picked up the mask and turned it over in his hands. A memory of the last time he had seen the doctor strapping it on stirred in his mind. He had helped him that night, had stuffed the beak with new dried flowers and herbs, added protection the Doctor had said, but his eyes had not looked convinced. Adam had tied the mask in place as the doctor's hands had trembled too much to secure it. He had looked pale, drawn, his movements were slow and pain creased his brow. 'Is anything the matter sir?' he had asked, but the doctor had reassured him, 'No Adam, I am just weary,' and he had smiled, clasped his bag firmly and stepped out into the cold night air. It was the last time Adam had seen him. As the following day was Sunday, Adam had spent the day in prayer and study, so it wasn't until the next morning that he received the news of his master's death. He listened numbly to the watchman. His master, having fallen sick whilst visiting a family, had stayed there to die rather than spread the disease any further. He had been a good man. Adam had nodded at a loss for words. His thoughts were racing. He had helped him with his mask. Had he touched his skin? Had his hands brushed his? He was sick; he must have known he was sick, yet he came to my house, I helped him to dress. Anger replaced fear, Adam had cursed and struck a wall hard with his fist.

That had been a terrible time. Adam had checked his body for signs of sickness for the next two weeks. Peering every morning and evening at any slight indication of a spot, rash or lump. He ventured out only for food supplies before retreating to his self-imposed exile. As the days passed and he stayed well, his anxiety had finally subsided only to be replaced by a new thought. A new fear. It was then that he had known they would come. Who else could they ask? Most of the qualified doctors had fled London and it was up to men such as himself to assume their burden. But Adam didn't want it. He did not want to die. He was afraid.

The mask placed back down onto the table, Adam opened up the leather bag again and stared. Inside was the black suit designed to protect him from the sickness in the air. It was slick with lard so that nothing could penetrate it; nevertheless, something had penetrated it he thought. Something deadly. Clenching his jaw, he placed the suit to one side pulling out a small leather-bound book. Inside he discovered lists of names and addresses all confined to the east side of London. Each name had either 'died' or 'survived' marked against it; the latter occurring with depressing infrequency. The handwriting was his master's and towards the end of the records were three entries which Adam understood were to be his first patients. Muttering a prayer, he traced the letters in each name whilst his other hand caressed the cross which he had been given by the vinegar man. He knew he had not the knowledge or skill to save them, so he pleaded silently that through him they may receive God's healing power. It was all he had to offer.

After a hasty, unappreciated supper, Adam began to dress carefully in his new clothes. Ingrained in the very fabric was a mixture of sweat, lard, smoke and faeces; Adam shuddered as it touched his virgin skin. After tugging on the moccasin boots which bit his toes, he picked up the mask. His own fingers trembled as he inhaled the sweet smell of herbs and dried flowers and it took him many attempts to fix it firmly into place. But, at last it was done. Pausing for a moment, Adam glanced around his room as if trying to hold it all in his memory and then, pocketing the silver cross, he stepped out into the darkness.

Taking a moment to allow his eyes to adjust to the gloom, Adam surveyed the everyday streets from the perspective of his new role. He had pounded these paths since childhood, but they had an unfamiliarity about them. He felt strange, so they felt strange. Would he always feel this way now? It was like a rebirth without any of the attendant joy. He wanted to be Adam again. Fingering the cross in an attempt to dispel futile thoughts he began picking his way through the miasma which wrapped itself around his black leather suit. His new cane tapped the cobbles, the sound masked by the ringing bells signalling the night's burials. Men, women and children all thrown into the hastily created pits on the edge of the city. Barbaric necessity? A device of convenience and not of conscience Adam reflected. Empty dwellings lined the narrow streets and windows remained unlit and unopened fuelling his claustrophobia. Notices nailed onto posts fluttered as a light breeze blew, their sombre dictations accessible to all.

Passing an old man wheeling a reeking cart towards the pits, Adam looked away. He had seen both the hope and fear in the old man's eyes as he sighted Adam's mask. He could almost verbalise the man's desperation that he, Adam, should become some sort of supernatural saviour assuaging the fears of the afflicted, making blind men see and crippled men walk.

Man and cart passed him, but the noxious fumes lingered causing him to adjust his mask. It was hot inside and sweat had already begun to collect on his brow threatening to run and sting his eyes. Breathing shallowly, he became aware of a tightness in his chest. His head pounded - the street swam. Leaning against a nearby wall he breathed deeply, forcing himself to inhale and exhale with increased regularity. His fingers wound tightly around the string of amber beads in his pocket, the edge of the cross piercing his flesh. The flow of blood brought him instant relief and a return to reality.

After taking a moment to check the address, he turned onto the path which led towards the docks where he observed, slashed across a door, a red cross still wet. This bloodied mark of death sealed the fate of the poor wretches confined inside. Outside a shiny buttoned watchman coughed a good evening holding an incongruously bright posy of flowers to his nose. Adam nodded back, slowing down as he passed him. A dim light could be seen between gaps in the boarded-up window. Surely the last light the inhabitants would see? Turning his head abruptly whilst uttering a short prayer, he pushed away the sight, resolute on reaching his destination.

The hem of his long coat trailed along the wet passageway. Wooden houses crowded into one another like drunks in a tavern. A mixture of rotten straw and faeces littered the street. The stench was unbearable, overpowering the meagre defence of the dried herbs and flowers. Finding the first door on his list, he stooped, stepping inside. A woman with worn hands and clothes led him into a small room lit by a sputtering tallow candle. With a trembling hand, she indicated a man unmoving on a makeshift bed then turned away unable to look. Moving self-consciously towards the patient he lifted the bed covers with his cane and glanced at the body beneath. He felt it everywhere, in every pore, in every corner of the room. Disease. Insufferable impotence. Guilt. He uttered a heartfelt prayer for the family whilst pressing the amber beads once more into his flesh. Shutting the door to the sound of sobs, he turned and nodded at the Watchman before he continued on his way

A few streets down, he paused to retrieve the leather-bound book from his pocket, to check the second address. As he did so, a tear fell smudging the dark ink.

He hastily brushed it away, pulling out a handkerchief, dragging it furiously across his eyes and crying aloud, 'I am in hell! What would you have me do Lord? I cannot help these people and they know it. I see it in their eyes. I am useless. You ask too much of me.' He sobbed with abandon, ceasing only when his passion had been sated.

Slumped on the ground exhausted but empty, Adam sat in the silence interrupted only by the intermittent ringing of the bells. After a moment he stood, dusting the detritus from his trousers whilst looking around him. In the excitement of the moment he had lost his way, but his internal compass soon reset and he mechanically moved towards his next destination. His eyes were dull and his steps were slow, but he was moving.

On this side of the borough the streets he walked through were busier yet less substantial. People clad in little more than rags, wandered in the spring evening or sat conversing with neighbours. Adam overhead snatches of their conversation as he made his way among them: all talk was about who had died or was dying. These were the poorest, the unwanted, those who could not afford to leave the city. The city which had been built by them was now consuming them. Their undernourished bodies bore scars and deformities, yet these were the survivors. For now.

The path was spongy underfoot with layers of household waste and what-else he dared not think. The mask was no protection against the odour and he felt bile rise in his throat which he hastily swallowed down. Surely no one chose to live like this? Houses here were little more than hovels, small, filthy and with as many occupants as the landlords could squeeze into them. Adam's breath quickened as he tried to focus on the task at hand, searching for the dwelling on his list. He found it at the end of a row, slightly tucked back from the rest. No-one was outside this house and the end of the street was dark and deserted. Shivering, Adam gently pushed the makeshift door. The lack of light wrong-footed him and stumbling, he fell onto an earthen floor which was distressingly damp and strewn with filthy straw. The smell of disease enveloped him, wrapping him in a tight embrace. Scrambling to his feet, he desperately wiped his hands on his trousers, attempting to regain his composure. Six pairs of eyes stared at him and he stared back. Becoming accustomed to the dark, he watched a girl of about 11 years approach him. ' Are you the doctor, Sir?' Her eyes looked at him imploringly, her wasted arms holding a stub of candle barely alight.

' Yes child, I am. Who is it that is sick?'

' Me sister, please can you help her?'

'Let me see her, I will do all that I can'.

Adam forced himself to look at the figure in the bed. Dear God it was a child, a child of no more than 5 years. A child who was so withered her skin barely covered her underdeveloped bones. He took in her gaunt face, sunken eyes, her ribs which protruded offensively from her chest and the glistening purple buboes - puss filled swellings - under her arms and in her groin. His throat and skin felt dry and itchy. He stuck out his hand for balance recoiling as it found a pile of greasy rags which fluttered to the ground like shrouds. Just audible were the burial bells which plucked at his nerves, unsteadying his legs. Must get out, mustn't touch her, must get out. Filth. Faeces. Disease. Don't let me touch her. Adam looked around the room at her young siblings, all malnourished, without adequate warmth or clothes. He knew for a certainty that they would all succumb to the disease. But not him, he had to get out. 'Can you help her Sir?'

He gasped, 'No…I…no, I am afraid I am too late.' His fingers rifled pockets for the comfort of the silver cross.

'Is it money? We got money.' She thrust a small pile of coins under his nose, but Adam recoiled from her. 'NO! No, I don't require payment, but I must, I must go I…'

Careful not to look at them, he pitched towards the door, when the girl grabbed his cloak tugging feebly at it. She was sobbing silently, tears drenching her face and mucous dripping from her nose. 'Please Sir, please help us They'll shut us in now won't they? They'll leave us to rot; we've no food, no nothin, please Sir, please.'

Adam fumbled for the door handle behind him and crashed back out into the street assaulted by the accusing cries of the girl. The cold air was a relief as it hit his fevered brow and he ran desperate to banish all he had just witnessed from his memory. He felt brutalised and the lifeless eyes of the child haunted him, concealing themselves within every subsequent thought. Uttering a prayer, he gave up half way through. What use was God to him? Where was he now? He wasn't to be found in these poor streets with the neediest of his flock. He had forsaken them and let the Devil in. He felt the sharpness of the cross in his pocket and jerked his fingers away recoiling at its warmth. He weaved along the streets heading for home; he had one more visit that night which would have to wait. I am ill, he told himself. His forehead burned feverishly and his eyes burned brightly. He began to laugh thinking of the watchman standing firm outside the house, overseeing the family's demise. 'Such shiny buttons,' he gasped, 'Such very shiny buttons' Hysterical, he laughed hopelessly.

Entering his home, Adam clawed off his clothes, scrubbed every inch of his body and sat motionless. He had lost more than his composure that night. In that hellish house, with the all but dead child, he had felt only the absence of God. Adam was not a learned man, but he had known there was a God just as there was air and water. But not now. Now there was only a pit of acid burning his insides, scorching away any belief he might have clung to. Now all was dark. He closed his eyes against the world and tried to sleep.

The next morning Adam rose and picked up his discarded clothing from the night before. Folding it carefully, he placed it back into the bag along with the leather-bound book, having first torn a page neatly from the back. He rested the fragile mask on top. He hummed to himself tunelessly as he washed his face. The fever from the night before had disappeared and was replaced with a new calm. Adam cleaned the fire place and laid it neatly ready for the evening. He swept the floor and washed up his supper plates. This done, he sat in his chair and looked through his window. It was a beautiful spring morning and a lone tree swayed gently, blossom just appearing to adorn the branches. As he watched, a sparrow flew near and chirpily strutted up and down a branch head cocked cheekily to one side until startled, it flew away. Taking pleasure from this simple scene Adam rested by the window, bathed in the warmth from the fledgling spring sun.

That afternoon, taking the paper he had torn from the book and some ink, Adam began to write. It was a laborious job as he was not a fluent writer, but he considered each word carefully to ensure it imparted his meaning. When he was finally finished, he folded it and left it on top of the leather bag. Satisfied, he smilingly ascended the stairs.

It was two days later when his door was finally forced open by a burly watchman making way for Councillor Andrews and Mr Thomas. Calling Adam's name they surveyed the neat kitchen. On top of the table, rested the leather bag and Mr Thomas passed the note which lay on top addressed to Councillor Andrews. Reading it silently, his mouth twisted, thin lips pressing bloodlessly together. Rearranging his features, he placed the letter securely into his pocket and turning to his colleague said, ' He is upstairs.' Obediently, Mr Thomas turned and ascended the stairs. Pushing open the bedroom door, he encountered Adam's body hanging from a rope. Mr Thomas stared, then righting an over turned stool balanced carefully and cut the body down. The smell of defecation nauseated him. Pulling a small sponge from his pocket he inhaled its vinegary aroma and hoped that Adam had not been diseased. As he passed through the doorway, his eyes caught sight of the silver cross he had bestowed upon Adam. It lay rejected upon the floor, the amber beads broken and scattered haphazardly. Pausing, he bent to retrieve the cross tucking it inconspicuously into his pocket.

Downstairs Councillor Andrews remarked that young men were constitutionally weak these days and that they could not be trusted to serve the public as selflessly as he and Mr Thomas had. In truth, he was shocked at Adam's heinous act. To renounce God was beyond his comprehension. He recalled the words Adam had written: 'God is no longer with me; I cannot hear his voice. I have nothing of value to offer those that need my help.

Without God's love, I cannot endure the trials of this world.' A fool, he thought, an irreligious heathen. Shaking him from his reverie, the watchmen arrived to collect the body. He instructed them to dispose of it in one of the many plague pits around the city. Retrieving the leather bag and mask, Andrews and Thomas stepped out into the street closing the door behind them.

JO SCARD

Before the pandemic, I could be found living on my family's fifty acres in regional Australia, baking banana bread, walking my dogs or running my for-good public relations and lobbying agency fiftyacres.com. After the pandemic arrived not a lot changed apart from failed attempts at sourdough and developing a healthy obsession for dystopian story-writing. I'm now spending much of my time dreaming up a beginning, middle and end for my final creative writing piece for the Master's degree at the University of Hull. Needless to say, it's a slightly more hopeful tale, at times even funny, about a trio who decamp to a cottage by the sea to wait out the pandemic and reinvent their lives. I hope you enjoy, and can relate to, this earlier piece, The Huggers.

THE HUGGERS

It was so gentle, as we moved slowly over and under. A deliciously soft rollercoaster cloud ride. Held up by soft unicorn coloured fairy floss, my fingers gently stroked her arm, moving down to hold her hand, I pulled her close and cocooned her in both of my arms.

Then, instantly, the noise of a bird outside broke through the cloud, and she was gone. As the grey light touched my pillow, I remembered we didn't do that. We didn't touch now.

Early on, I remembered that in the before times we hugged. We kissed. We held hands. We did not listen to sad playlists on the couch while reading about how, because some humans ate pangolins, or maybe bats, the world might end.

Endless numbers of dead people. Scientists in my lounge room. How many sick today?

I remember that in the before times I would think about online dating and park walking with my four-legged. Or I'd be on the bus and catch the eye of a beautiful stranger. Embarrassed, I'd look away and back down at my phone, scrolling, not stopping. Brushing up against them as I alighted, arriving at the cafe I'd wrap my arms around my friend before we had tea. We could see each other's smiles. Those were the days, my friends.

Before this all started it was what I didn't tell my psych Agnes that I wrestled with the most. I should have told her everything, but it was too late now. Agnes had gone offline.

In Agnes's absence, the interwebs told me to start something called morning pages. I did them in the afternoon. It's basically writing.

I wrote about all the dead women, once loved, that I could no longer touch.

Or never could touch, because they were gone before I was here.

About my ability to go deep into rabbit holes and not come up.

I hadn't seen Agnes in over six weeks now we were staying in. I missed our talks. The glass of water. The box of tissues.

I was all out of sorts. This inside thing was like a cat amongst the pigeons in my head. Wash your hands. Distance. Mask yourself.

I have headbanging loneliness. Heartbreaking sadness.

And, so, it began. Was it meshugas, frenzy, lunacy or insanity? I convince myself there is sense in endless Google searches, it's fine, isn't it?

Thinking about it, it probably started, innocently, with my beguiling rendition of Celtic ballad Danny Boy which I sang to my dog, Sam, each day. The song was played at my Great Grandmother's funeral, so the story went. I hug Sam, but he just sits there.

It was the seventh week in. And it spiralled from there.

It was easy to go down deep into those holes. There was nothing much else to do.

Bad place the interwebs.

And there was a lot of time to do it in, now.

It was either find the best recipe for pantry staples, or decide what eye shadow palette to buy, with the complete and full realisation that it would take weeks to arrive and that I would not want to wear eyeshadow by the time it got here, anyway. But, in that moment, I was driven.

There had been a lot of those moments. Delayed satiety was so unsatisfying.

I knew that I had just left one world and entered a new one, and in this new world, I did not yet know how to move. So I kept Googling.

The wise man on the TV said 'Young people are staring down the barrel here.'

'But, we will get through this,' he said.

You're a fucking liar, I said.

On the other side of my grief is a world I knew nothing about, a world I had no way of responding to.

So, I waited without optimism, with no expectations, prodding my eyes open after I woke, letting this new world slowly form around me.

I keep swimming in the dark cesspit of the interwebs along with the doomsday preppers. I jump in, and it is one deep, dark pool.

I had two options, according to Google. Either deep dive where the preppers are or get ready for the Zombie Apocalypse, which I found out is an actual thing.

The New Yorker, which I still had an online subscription to, wrote all about it. Some fancy pants, dripping in gold Americans had made their way to New Zealand to prepare for the apocalypse. They are actually there waiting. There are pictures on the New York Times.

Maybe this was it, and the apocalypse was happening right now? They were right.

I need answers. I need to know: is this doomsday?

So, I keep searching.

Stumble on Sylvia. Always loved Sylvia. Always. She's just like me, beautiful, and on the obsessive side, and I find out she had a ouija board. Would be quite handy when you're staying in, I thought' having a board like that. Her big, brute husband person got her into it. He was an arsehole poet Wikipedia says.

They say it was the thing what did her in, in the end, that board. Made her mad, then she gassed herself. Stuck tape around the kitchen doors to save the children, lucky for them, then put a pillow in front of the oven. It was good she thought it all through. Hard to think about the kids when you're in that deep. Google says going that way is supposed to be painless.

My self-destructive fascination made me do it. I'd be home for a while, so, why not, so I ordered a board too, just like hers. It arrived in that brown box with the orange smile. I thought about doing an Instagram unboxing video but didn't. Didn't want to be judged by my one hundred and three followers. They might think I'd gone crazy.

After all that, it didn't work. So I went back to jigsaw puzzles.

As someone who used to consider herself a bit of a social butterfly, it was hard to accept the fact that I was loving this inside time, and I wished it would never end. I was in love with this discombobulated sense of time in parenthesis.

I had dreams. So many dreams. Just like that cyborg I listened to on TED who is colour blind, lives in New York, Neil Harbisson, and has a microphone attached to his brain through his skull, for real, and dreams in colours and hears things he sees. Neil says taxis sound like limes. Imagine that. Problem is there aren't any taxis, so I thought Neil would be a bit sad about that. They call it synesthesia, what he has.

My dreams aren't as good as Neil's, they're more like that app that superimposes forest scenes over your head in muted technicolour. But they're pretty good.

Back on Instagram, people either recommend fairy tales or pandemic novels.

Influencers suggest I breathe. Intermittent fast. Stretch. Use bottles of laundry detergent for weights. Go keto. Drink more water. The news says the consumption of wine has gone up.

I read a few of those pandemic novels on Kindle. They are vatic with accounts of injustice, suffering and farce.

If we'd been smart just last year, we might have guessed we were heading here, but we didn't know, because we thought we were different. We were real, and that was a book. And it was only last Christmas. Time flys. Not fun.

From memory, when I was at school, we always used to think we were better than those dystopian stories. It was a dark, scary novel. It was make-believe.

I convince myself that when it's all over, if it ever is, there will be make-believe again. We'll know imagination once more, and we will write our own words. It will be called post-dystopia, maybe. Whoever works that one out will win the Booker, for sure, I reckon.

But back in real life, when the next thing comes, maybe it really will be preparing for the Zombies, because what else is there? Zombies are as bad as it can get, surely? But we'll be ready. Nothing's silly now.

I know that I'm talking to myself. But that's OK. There's no-one else to talk to. There is no-one other than the dog to hear.

And I say: The people who come after us, they will have to make their own way out of this blind alley, and into the next one. They'll find a small gap to escape, but it will lead them to another hell, another Catch-22, from which they must escape. Just like we are trying to do right now, to escape, right?

I don't have an answer to my question.

Early on, around week three, when it seemed like it might be the last day of the world, day after day it might have been the last day, I started transcribing those inside brain words. Furtively. Futilely.

And I read.

And experimented.

Much later, I go back to the board. I play with a Guardians of the Galaxy hologram torch. Hoping they will take me to the happy place with children playing in playgrounds. Hoping they would let me talk to those joyful dead women. They don't.

One of the funny things, if you could call any of this funny because it really isn't, but I was past knowing funny from un-funny, was that, now, as we were all in, we had become morphed into two-dimensional strangers on flat screens.

I keep watching as people let down their inhibitions and confess the craziness of the in, the mad things they are doing, openly, without fear. Even Michelle Obama confessed. Things when they were out that they would never have said.

And we see things we would never have seen in the out time. The sex toy in the distance on the table. The naked children. Pajamas when they stand up. Brett Easton Ellis on the bookshelf. You would never have taken that physiotherapist as into transgressive snuff. She was so prim. Well ironed. Tidy low key makeup. Was it a message or a mistake.

I kept transcribing. Words spilling.

I recall the climate crisis. What crisis when it's doomsday already? Doomsday is the now crisis.

Who cares about the polar bears when we might die if someone, somewhere eats the only mammals capable of true and sustained flight.

I find solace in those preppers. I get them. They feel like my people.

In the face of civilisation collapse prepping was all I could do, wasn't it?

My reading tells me that in times of plague, boundaries break down. It dawns on me that hasn't all of human history been one partial apocalypse after another? The dinosaurs and that meteorite, ice age, rats, plague, wars, influenza, the internet, climate change. When I contemplate this, I experience what seems like the correct emotions: grief, fear, anxiety.

Are these in brain things madness? How would I know now? I can't calibrate madness. There is nothing to measure it by anymore.

What I love about this in time, this lazaretto, is the feeling of invisibility. It is quiet. But not my brain. My brain is like trance music, one hundred and fifty-five beats per minute.

I am mesmerised by the rhythms of this temporal sequestration. I try to slow it down but can't. I play fantasy hockey. I watch Hamilton three times on Disney.

I Google 'how to hug' and it comes up with 498,000,000 results in 0.47 seconds. I practice in the mirror but it doesn't help.

I want to think that impromptu encounters will once again be the rule. That I won't be scared if I'm not in.

I know, as the threat of the thing those scaly mammals brought, or whatever it was that brought it, continues, we may never have that out life again.

I learn a new word: omakase (任せる. I will leave it up to you.

Well, I can't leave it to others, can I? There are no others. It's all up to me now.

I read about the posthumans, the transhumans, the extropians, the immortalists, the postgenderists, the AI-ists that are all wired to try and answer the question. But they too have failed. No-one can plan now.

I read that in Greek, the word for private shares the same root as the word for idiot. We are all fools.

I have morbid thoughts. I look for how others end it. It's easy to find in the darkness of the web. I have nothing to go to, nothing. I have no evidence it will end.

I read that Hollywood blog, Goop and it tells me to breathe. I hadn't done it properly before, although I've lived twenty-four years. A Vogue story says I do not have to write the next bestselling novel. I do not have to become a goddess. I don't need to start a podcast. Yet, what else is there to do but that, so I should at least try to become a goddess or write a novel. But I run out of energy, so I sleep.

I become curious with this time and decide I should have no agenda other than to experience the thing. Still, my brain keeps going at break speed. What if I just live for the sake of living?

I turn on my laptop, and The New Yorker tells me what to read, watch, cook, and listen to in the in. What it doesn't tell me is how I can keep inside my head smooth like my exxy caviar eye cream I used pre the in. My head is all dried up.

Before the in, I dreamt I lived in New York, but I'm happy not to be there. Long dead lists. War graves on a nearby island. Good I'm here, I think.

I download twenty-two fitness apps and try p.volve, Kinrgy, The Class, skipping rope, barre and pilates. I alternate between one hundred and twenty minutes or zero movement each day. I tell myself I need rest days. Goddess goals wax and wane.

When this confinement began, enforced isolation from a zoonotic catastrophe, we didn't know that we were taking part in a terrible, frightful laboratory experiment, which would be a test on our capacity to bear loneliness.

Do I pull out my hair? Do I smash my head against the walls of my cage? Do I, locked up, scream and moan?

This new solitude is hard. It seems more like hide and seek than shelter.

When was the last time someone walked through my door?

Would I ever delight in the mess, the smells of touch again?

Intimacy is a word I use until one day I stop because it now feels like gobbledygook. The word has been removed from my dictionary.

I have memories.

I remember that dream sequence from that movie where Keanu Reeves runs with horror through an entirely humanless city. Those streets terrified me. This is it, real-time.

Or it's a 23-19 Monsters Inc. sort of scene, where Sully and Mike avoid running into trouble at the Scare Factory after a sock is left on the shoulder of one of the professional floor scarers. Only the sock can't be removed.

This thing has its own time. The scientists say that it's been around for millions of years and has morphed into a new form and is now circulating in us. Circling and breaking us apart.

On the rare occasion I go out, I am careful.

I don't want to touch anything. Every object, every thing, every surface is covered with invisible ink which reads 'you are all going to die'.

And two-leggeds, they are the carriers. How could you ever be safe around a two-legged again?

When putting out the garbage one night I see them up above, on the sixth floor. It's dark and there are curtains but I can see six or seven of them. They are touching.

Back inside, on the settee, I stumble. Across them. Down hundreds of holes. After decoding their name I find them: The Huggers. I am accepted into the group after lots of questions. I'm breathing fast. Then sleep.

Things change almost as suddenly as they fell apart.

Week thirty-seven I receive a direct message from one of them about attending their meet-up. It throws me.

After weeks, or is it months, of receiving notices of cancellations and closures, this is the first invitation I have received from what might be the future, and I find my reaction to this invitation disturbing.

A sadness, the kind you experience when a friend is moving away, and you wave goodbye knowing you will not call, just DM, if that.

This is a reaction to the in that I am slow to contend with, even ashamed of.

That I want it to stay. It suits me. I suit it.

The invitation reads:

We don't know each other, I live on the 6th floor. A few of us have arranged a get together this Sunday to hug. There are risks involved, but we think it's worth it. Entry strictly upon presentation of a negative test and wearing gloves and mask. RSVP by 4pm Friday. Enter at your own risk and fines are paid by each attendee should police arrive.

I wait for twenty-four hours, then say yes. Can't hurt. Well, I could die, but apart from that. What will I wear?

A few more days of cupboard meals.

I exfoliate all the dead skin off my legs in the shower and wash my hair with volumising shampoo and conditioner. I worked out I hadn't washed it for eleven weeks, but it didn't look like it.

I decide to wear jeans I'd ordered online and an oversized sweater.

I apply some lip gloss, grab my keys, close the door and walk to the lift, reach out with my gloved hand and press the down button.

Those breathing blog posts I've read don't help much.

I get out of the lift on the sixth floor and walk towards the stranger's apartment. I knock gently and hear the sound of footsteps as someone approaches the door.

It opens. I smell incense. The girl is wearing a rainbow-hued t-shirt with a unicorn picture embossed on it.

'I'm on the eleventh floor,' I say.

'Come in, I'm so glad you could make it,' her eyes smile, 'we're just getting started.'

KATIE BENNETT

Katie Bennett has always been pretty keen on writing. In fact, for a long time, her dad thought she would make a great journalist. Unfortunately, she wasn't that creative so she decided to have a go at writing fiction instead. She particularly enjoys writing about women, and how political, social, and religious expectations shape everything from the clothes we wear to the medical diagnoses we receive. Katie has spent time working as a bookseller, a secondary school English teacher, and a content writer, although not necessarily in that order. Her writing companion is a dog named Sherlock, who lives up to his namesake. When her head isn't stuck in a book, Katie enjoys getting outdoors, losing the odd game of badminton, and pretending she knows how to use her telescope.

THE LINES WE CROSS

It didn't occur to me that I was a criminal. Not at first. Not until I was strung out on anxiety waiting for the police to arrive. You see, time's a funny thing. It warps and stretches in the most inconvenient ways. And always when you'd rather it would gallop past, fast as a filly.

That November? Time meandered from tick to tock accompanied by an almost constant patter of rain.

It was a Tuesday when the police turned up. The day when Sarah had P.E. Every week, she'd search frantically for her kit. Her anger has always been a tangible thing, and it was no different back then. You could feel frustration radiating from her like heat shimmers as she tore through her wardrobe. I'd watch from the doorway. Looking back, I wasn't a particularly soothing presence.

"If you tidied —"

"You're a shit mum." Her eyes would spit fire whenever we clashed. "You're supposed to help me."

Anna was different. She would glide past us both like a wraith. No one guessed her blazer hid jagged tears in her pale flesh.

They walked themselves to school. It wasn't far.

I had stripped and remade the beds until the warmth of jasmine and vanilla dallied in the air. Until my arms protested and sweat decorated my hairline. Just to pass the time.

It wasn't unusual for the hum of traffic to be interrupted by sirens. Only days before, an ambulance had arrived at the house opposite. Faces had gathered in top floor windows to watch as Fishy Freddy was stretchered away, swaddled like a baby in the paramedic's red blanket. We called him that, in our house at least, because every now and then he would arrive at our door, chest puffed out, and hand over a carrier bag full of freshly caught fish. I used to cover them in flour and fry them, or turn them into fish cakes, but by then they were going straight in the bin. They'd reeked of ammonia one time, and I didn't like to risk it after that.

I was about to start the ironing. Having school-age kids leaves you with a constant pile of laundered uniforms to de-crinkle. I used to take in ironing when Anna was young. That's the thing about kids, isn't it? You do anything to put food on the table.

There was a knock on the door. It was what all that soupy time had been leading up to. My stomach dive bombed towards my toes. I practiced an expression of surprise and innocence in the mirror and tugged my jumper into place.

Turns out I didn't need to practice. I'd expected the two detectives, one in a sagging grey suit and the other in carefully tailored navy. The riot van was a different matter. The England rugby team could have a formed a defensive line or two from the men who blocked off the driveway.

"Can I help you?"

"We're looking for Darren Pullman."

You see, time might dangle your sanity on a whisker for a while, but it always snaps back. And it was those spikes of activity that were the real fuckers. It was time to give my visitors my best performance.

It started with a phone call.

"Where are you?"

Darren. His demand held a familiar thread of urgency. I spent a lot of time rolling my eyes when he called. And his calls became more frequent the longer we were divorced.

"At home." Lorries rumbled at the other end of the phone. "Are you still in France?" "Martin's been arrested."

I muted Jeremy Kyle and his vitriolic guests. The show was a staple of my mornings. Chocolate chip shortbread and a bitter, black tea dulled the keen edge of jobless boredom. I had been looking for a part-time job, but a long stint as a housewife, plus two children who were still school age, left me an undesirable prospect.

"How do you know?" I wanted to be sure before I gave in to the squirming panic uncoiling in my abdomen. The last time I'd seen Martin, I'd still been married. He'd met me and Darren at the services near Doncaster. Three Burger King coffees had been cooling on the table when he stood to greet us. He'd shaken our hands like it was a business meeting. He was compact, with a firm, dry grip and a fox-like energy. We chatted over the burnt, cheap coffee and walked away with a bag full of cash.

"Liz called."

It was confirmation enough. Liz was Martin's wife. If he was a fox, she was a deer. I had never seen her without her little boy, Jack. He was a ruddy-cheeked fire cracker with almond shaped eyes and the round, flat face associated with Downs Syndrome. Liz had once confessed over a glass of wine that she would have had an abortion if she'd known. But I'd never seen her look at her son with anything other than a glow of love and pride.

"I need your help."

I heard the tic-tic of an indicator at the other end of the line. My eyes strayed to the window. I thought about the kids. My mind came to rest on the pile of twenties in the safe. I couldn't say no.

"Just tell me what you want me to do."

The estate agent's office would have looked right at home in an eighties police drama. Remember the one where the policeman was sent back in time? Anyway, the estate agent surveyed me with scepticism from behind her desk. Chipped fuchsia nails hovered over a yellowing keyboard. An irregular dripping eroded my nerves as water fell from stained ceiling tiles and into a tangerine coloured bucket below. Around it, a creeping white stain was expanding across the charcoal carpet like the tide across volcanic sand.

"And you're his ex-wife?" A thick, drawn on eyebrow arched in disbelief.

"Yes." I did my best to look harmless. "I just need to borrow the key to his flat." "To get his passport?"

"He's a lorry driver. He needs to be in France tomorrow."

"And you're taking it to him?"

"I'm meeting him halfway." My hands were curled together on my lap. I hoped she couldn't see how white my knuckles were. The police could explode through the door at any moment and catch me in my lie.

"Absolutely not." The woman's lips – painted the same colour as her nails - curled upwards.

"Call him." Almost an hour had passed since Darren had rang. "Please. It's important."

The estate agent obliged with a flick of her ponytail. Her face crinkled with displeasure as the conversation progressed, only for her to hang up with a sigh. I got the impression that she wouldn't let any ex of hers within five miles of her home if she had the choice, let alone hand over the keys. She retreated to a back office to retrieve them for me. It was once I had the white envelope in my hand that fear really set in.

There are areas in every town that make you wince when you enter them. Grimsby is no exception. The charred husk of a Corsa adorned the car park of flats where Darren lived. The building's residents had adopted a dress code of tracksuit bottoms, baseball caps, and disintegrating trainers. They prowled the corridors, twitching with boredom. For once, I was more worried about the arrival of sirens than being mugged in the corridor.

The flat itself had been decorated through a sepia lens. Furniture polish, citrus, and the faint burn of bleach perfumed the air. No trace of the man I had married lingered in open plan living space. You'd expect a photo of his daughter, Charlotte, or a couple of books, wouldn't you? Perhaps a bottle of whisky on the counter, or a scattering of magnets on the fridge from holidays past? But Darren's always been tidy. Too tidy. The constant hoovering used to drive me and my girls mad. The minimalism made it easy to find the phones though. All five of them were hibernating in the tea towel drawer under precisely folded pieces of cloth.

The handsets were cheap with large buttons. The kind you give to elderly relatives. Nokia, Motorola, Samsung. Each was a different make and model. I slipped off the smooth plastic backs and prized out the batteries with my nails. Shaking fingers snapped each SIM card in two. I swept the components into three separate food bags that I found in a

cupboard. It looked suspicious as hell when I retreated to my car with those in hand. Swollen raindrops splattered against the windscreen as I clutched the steering wheel. I could see the top of a police car about halfway down the street. Its lights were dark.

I couldn't tell if there were officers secreted inside. My heart quivered. For all I knew, they were already in the apartment building. They could have taken the stairs as I descended in the lift. They could be heading back down, handcuffs out, as my Qashqai rumbled to life around me.

I don't remember much of my drive through town. Suffice to say that every wailing siren, or glimpse of day-glow yellow and blue, sent bolts of electric anxiety through me. And all the while I tried not to think of my girls, who would, no doubt, be staring out of steamy classroom windows, looking at the charcoal smudge of sky as they pondered maths and science.

I found myself as driftwood on the shore. Waves crashed against the sea wall, frothing and foaming at the concrete that contained them. Lampposts danced drunkenly in the salty air overhead. On the passenger seat, my three food bags of contraband burned hot as coals, demanding my attention. I had to get rid of them. I longed to throw them into the churning, weak-tea coloured water and be done, but the instructions had been clear: every piece should go in a different bin.

I had two hours until I had to be home for the girls. It wasn't a lot of time to find twenty bins. I was particularly reluctant to use two in a row. The walk along the promenade and back left my hair plastered to my cheeks. The weather made every passerby seem dubious, and I couldn't shake the feeling that some undercover agent was following me. The seafront has, to this day, an abundance of bins, yet I only managed to rid myself of a few bits of SIM card and three batteries.

My next stop was a small retail park with a McDonald's and a KFC. I bought myself a couple of coffees and emptied the scalding contents into a flowerbed; I was jittery enough without the caffeine. I put a handset in each of the empty cups, secured the plastic lids, then binned them at opposite ends of the car park.

The molten panic I'd felt since Darren first called began to cool, leaving me with a background buzz of dread and a twist of tentative excitement. I hadn't been pulled over. No one had stopped me. I was getting away with it. I drove to a supermarket, stopped on the high street, and took a blustery walk through the cemetery. All the while, the windscreen wipers were swishing away the seconds until I had to be home.

There was a single phone remaining.

It was almost three o'clock, and the school bell rang at five past. I was only around the corner from the school's main entrance. It was an impulse to park as near to the gates as possible and pick up the girls. Traffic was sluggish. I drummed my fingers against the wheel as I crept between parked cars, refusing to give way.

Fate offered me a spot close to the gates. A bin squatted by a sign announcing the school's specialism: performing arts. Sarah and Anna had certainly learned those skills in excess, if their behaviour at home was anything to go by. I hopped out of the car as the first students trickled onto the path. Four exaggerated strides carried me past waiting parents. I slipped the food bag into the bin, my bulky winter coat shielding my actions from view. Not that I was of particular interest to those around me.

My children were horrified and delighted in equal measure to find me standing on the street. I should qualify: any pleasure they displayed was likely due to the fact they didn't have to walk home. Embarrassment was evident on their faces. No teenager, whether eleven or fifteen, wants their bedraggled mother turning up at school unannounced when she doesn't have the good grace to wait inside the car. They made sure I understood that as we drove home. It made me flush with love and guilt.

I called Darren while I made the girls' tea.

"It's sorted."

"You're sure?" Apprehension gave his voice a higher pitch.

"All five." I leant against the kitchen counter, listening to the girls bicker over the remote. "Now what?"

"The police will come, I think."

"Here?" Something low in my gut clenched.

"I'm still registered there, but they might go to the flat. They might be there now." And then the waiting began. Time turned to taffy. All stringy and sticky. It wrapped round my guts and choked the air from my lungs until my limbs trembled at smallest noise. I cleaned and cooked and practiced my script, readying my nerves for the knock that would come on that Tuesday morning in November.

"We're looking for Darren Pullman."

"Darren?" I met the hazel gaze of the detective in the navy suit. "He hasn't lived here for months."

"Darren's your husband?" Grey suit asked the question.

"We're divorced." I sighed and ran my fingers through my hair. "You better come in." I held the door wide. Grey suit entered. The detective in navy waved the lineup of riot police back to the van. The neighbours would be watching. It gave me a strange feeling of satisfaction.

We took seats in the living room. They declined cups of tea. Navy suit seemed irritated by the anti-climax. He clasped his hands in his lap and fidgeted. Those hazel eyes swept the room, pausing on the pictures of the girls on the mantel. I swallowed down the icy spike of fear that wedged itself in my throat and smiled.

"We want to talk to Darren in relation to some ongoing enquiries." Grey suit had taken charge. Deep creases lined his forehead and met at the corners of his eyes. "Did he give you this address?" I hoped my scowl was convincing. "I'll bloody kill him. What's he done?"

They declined to comment.

"Do you know where your ex-husband is, Miss —"

"McCall. Miss McCall." I probably should have offered a first name. "And, no. I'm sorry. He's a truck driver." I knew exactly where he was. He was sat in McDonalds with his daughter, eating breakfast. He did the same every Tuesday. Then he dropped her off at college. "Are you sure I can't get you a drink?"

"Do you have a number we can reach Mr Pullman on?" Navy suit seemed out of patience.

"I can call his daughter if you like? Leave a message? Darren and I aren't on speaking terms, you see?" Was lying to the police perverting the course of justice? I thought it was. I was pretty sure people went to prison for that.

"Please." Grey suit responded. I saw him frown at his colleague when he thought I was looking at my phone screen.

"Charlotte? Hi! How are you?" I held a finger up to the policemen as I nodded along to Charlotte's response. "Listen, darling. The police are looking for your dad —" I pulled a face, trying to indicate that Charlotte was upset. "No, of course it's nothing to worry about." I shrugged at my guests."Could you let him know sweetheart? Thanks ever so much." I ended the call.

"I'm sure he'll be in touch, but if there's anything else."

They thanked me for my time and left. I slumped in the hallway and sobbed. I was a criminal. I'd destroyed evidence. Lied to the police. Spent the proceeds. I was an accomplice to Darren and Martin's crimes, no matter that I hadn't physically helped. I fought for breath. I flung my phone at the wall. It clattered to the laminate floor and skipped in the direction of the kitchen.

"What happens now?" I could hear the whoosh of traffic at the other end of the line. Somewhere, a siren sounded. I picked at the skin around my nails as I waited for Darren to reply.

"I go see my solicitor and hand myself in." The familiar urgency his voice usually held had drained away.

"Just like that?"

"It's the best way."

"What about me?" It felt selfish to ask when he could be facing prison. But by then, I knew that was a risk for me, too.

"They might want to talk to you, but I won't tell them anything." Darren sighed. It was easy to imagine him racing around town in his Golf, frantically destroying evidence and ironing out alibis. "You don't know anything."

"I don't know anything." I repeated the words over and over in the days that followed.

I've wondered on more than one occasion how I got through that November. The house has certainly never been as clean since. And I've never spent so much money, so fast. On stupid things, too. Just to get rid of those notes in the safe. The girls had a great Christmas that year, for sure. Me? I was still waiting for the sirens to stop outside my door. All for the cash that comes from a few smuggled cigarettes.

SARAH WILKS

From being a child I have always been fascinated by language and its development in society. I found 'magic' in words and attribute this to my favourite childhood stories: The Nightingale and the Rose, The Magic Faraway Tree and Where the Wild Things Are. Each one of these 'tales' have been re-read throughout my life and although meant as childhood stories an adult reader sees so much more - a complete contrast to the innocent reading of a child. Despite the fact that the words have not changed, the response to the text changed completely.

Both my pieces are inspired from texts that I have read but that I felt a strong connection to. "The Room" was inspired by "The Yellow Wallpaper" and "The Door" by "The Woman in Black". I am currently working on a young adult piece as part of my final piece and hope that it will fit in to part of my novel. As a secondary teacher I have found that reading for pleasure is becoming a lost art so I decided to (attempt) to write a novel that was relevant, relatable and covered topics that are important to young people.

THE ROOM

Depressing, harrowing and lifeless, my soul was empty. They left me here without looking back.

I sat looking through the window. This was the main feature of the room and is supposed to be the most 'uplifting' part. The wooden frame hung like the fellow willow trees just beyond its shattered glazed glass. Funny looking trees the willow trees aren't they? They are supposed to represent nurture and protection and symbolise strength and stability. What a sick joke. I wondered whether they were purposely planted there as they represent change too.

The frame's paint cracked and sizzled in the dusk's glow, as the last ray of sun attempted to shine its hopeful ray into the room. I sat there for some time eagerly watching the wildlife outside running up the trees in search of food, afraid to be seen, skipping away from the open spaces. Had they seen me watching? My shoulders dropped. Even nature was repulsed by me. Like everyone else it too couldn't wait to get away from me. I sat there for what felt like hours as the sky turned black. I moved away from the window and I could see that the once white walls of the room had faded, turned into a deep musky yellow colour. The once lavish furniture was covered with throws to hide the thread bare patches. The once luxurious bed with its tall wooden poles in each corner as though each was on duty to protect the person inside, were now chipped and covered in scratches. The once healthy mind of mine searched for comfort and I jumped on the bed. The basic sheets were crisp and clean and the old itchy blanket provided enough weight to make me feel safe.

I lay there looking at the walls; they were covered in fragments of archaic wallpaper, which moved with each blink. Twisting and convulsing patterns pawed out with each eye movement and the blistered paintwork was almost breathing in rhythmic time with mine. We were connected, I was focused, and I was now calm. My mind tried to decipher what the patterns were. Swirls and twists moved across the wall in a whispering dance. Flowing elegantly directing me to the corner of the room and to something that I hadn't noticed. Deep in the corner, almost hidden, was a worn chair the seat was imprinted suggesting a person was still sat in it, a single occupant just like me, looking at the lone seat made me cry. The haunting thought lingered in the air and I started to choke on my tears.

The worn bed frame had been pierced, jerked and masked by the falling wallpaper, and was saturated in a thick layer of varnish and dust that suffocated the once grand solid wooden frame. You could see where they had tried to fix it and make it like new. Dented varnish with bubbles of dust traced the frame of the bed. The varnish was simply a mask trapping the years of grime deep inside. A quick and simple fix, a simple, shiny surface to cover the damage. If only it was that easy for me.

Pointlessly lying there, I felt numb. I traced the ends of my fingers, circling around with my index finger, then my little finger, then moving my thumb across the middle of my palm then starting again to repeat the pattern over and over again. Eyes closed tight trying to regulate my breathing. My head nodding in rhythm with my heart beat. I couldn't stop thinking about that night and I gagged. Flashing images of the events raced in my mind and it silently screamed in horror as it regurgitated the one memory I couldn't bear. The memory that I thought I had dealt with-until last night.

My eyes again fixated on the crumbling ceiling moved down to scan onto the radiator, which once worked and filled the room with its warmth and safety. But like the rest of the room has now become old and broken and again in an attempt at restoration the thick layers of paint peeled and cracked inside the rails. The hollow bubbles of the paint look ready to burst; some already peeling revealing the worn industrial orange metal. The colour darkened in between the cylinders where it was clear the cleaner couldn't get in to clean it properly - like it was riddled with disease. Each molecule of dirt mutated and stuck in the hollows. A lone spider peered through, its long legs swarming through cracks, using body fluid pressure from its blood to slowly move. Like me the spider cannot close its eyes. It too does not sleep, it too has to reduce its activity level and lower its metabolic rate to conserve energy. That is why they put me here.

They said I needed to rest and that I needed to get away from everyone.

It felt unnatural almost mechanical and robotic. Just like the spider I had daily cycles of activity that I had to do. I had to remember to breathe. I had to remember to move my face. I didn't want them to think I had had a stroke again. I couldn't bear the disappointment on their faces when they had realised that it was just my face. My grey eyes sunk into the back of my titled head, and my mouth hung low at each side and it had been that way for so long that if I did have the courage to smile the pain would be too horrific. My face was framed with limp knots of hair that seemed to be stuck awkwardly around my scalp. I had continual red jewelled bits of dry blood embedded around my finger nails, the remnants of the last few months of anxiously picking and biting at my skin. The dark purple veins are still prominent all around my neck and I don't recall the last time that I brushed my teeth. I traced my tongue along them trying to move away the layers of yellow plaque. I had stopped noticing the smell of my body months ago. But I could still breathe. I just had to remember to. The spider had hidden herself so I couldn't see her from where I was lying. My eyes desperately searched but she had gone.

Lifting my head off the pillow didn't work either so I tried to focus on something else. My eyes were drawn toward the door.

Each solid panel of wood was joined together with a gold beaded trim, like something from the 60s. The gold handle, which matched the gold beading on the rest of the door, had blisters of wear and tear and a small lock that I had no key for. The door offered me protection, behind it I could do whatever I wanted. I was invisible and safe.

But it was always closed. They said if I stopped trying to attack that I would be able to come out. But that wasn't true. They knew from the state of me when I arrived that I was harmless. It made me wonder exactly what my family told them. Did they even care that I was here trapped behind this throwback door, the door that took away my choices. I used to see doors as a new beginning, moving from one part of life to another, where new possibilities and opportunities could be reached like some metaphorical, spiritual gateway to my happiness and my dreams and ambitions. Not now. This door was the keeper of my freedom, this thin layer of wood kept me imprisoned.

I studied the oak pattern in each panel each wooden fingerprint started to move in unison, like a swarm of ants, militant, marching up and down. Not stopping, not looking back just relentlessly, repeating their mundane task over and over again. Up down, around the groove across the beading then back in form. Then again up down around the beading and back in form tracing the oblong circular patterns of the oak's identity. My eyes started to blink and I saw the handle start to drop. They were here.

Looking up at the ceiling once more, I could see the stout woman as her thick hands cautiously opened the door and ordered me to stay on the bed. Lying there with my hands by side as instructed, I followed her with my eyes. Her face changed when she looked at me. I saw fear in her eyes. I wanted to scream out that it was an accident, but I didn't. I was good. I did as I was told. They said to just behave, and listen to what they are asking of me and be honest and it will all be over. Over, as if they would let me go. She left the tray of food on the small plastic table by the window and took the other untouched tray away.

'You need to start eating' she said.

'Try and get some rest and I will be back later'.

It is funny in places like this they don't wear a uniform. It is as if they want to seem more human to us.

I know I'm not the only one here- even though that is what they told me. I hear things at night, banging and footsteps. They tell me that there are no rooms above me, but I know that is a lie. I hear a voice, sometimes I try and communicate. But when I do the noise stops.

Lowering my eyes I saw a picture of a forest with a family taking part in a picnic. The sight of this gave me hope. Hope of freedom and to potentially be reunited with my family. To be reunited with my mind. The father figure stood playfully with open arms, as if to receive the child running towards him. Was that me in the background hiding behind a tree in the picture, hidden away as always from the fun, I threw my head back on the bed. I needed to escape this hell hole. But at the same time it had me. I could see my face slowly edging its way into the walls. I was trapped.

THE DOOR

As he approached the last road towards his destination, the full beam of his car gleamed through the coastal road, his stomach churned at the thought of walking through that door. He didn't know why he felt this way, but he knew it was the evil that called him home. He was powerless. Oppression weighed heavy on his shoulders. The melancholy black, thick sky hung so low it was as though it was pushing him, directing him. He could not explain it. Even the tide was edging its way surrounding him, forcing him in one direction, the house. This was the only way to get rid of his psychosis. He wanted his life back and he needed his life back. Losing everything had finally forced him to wake up.

The day his wife left was the day he started to seek love in whiskey and the pub. He found solace in the drink and the people at the pub quickly became his comfort. He then lost his job at the firm, although they had kept him on as long as they could, he just could not function so they 'parted ways' giving him a huge pay out if he went quietly. Luckily he was mortgage free and his wife had just wanted a quick escape and did not pursue a legal battle. His two children stopped coming around, after his daughter caught a serious illness from the state of his house and ended up being in hospital for weeks. After that and several unanswered called they eventually gave up too.

He had desperately lost his way and he didn't recognise the person he was becoming. His self-reassurance was that he was just enjoying himself. He tried desperately to find that missing piece from his soul. She had left him and he had no idea why. He was a good husband and a model father. Day after day he went through their life together over and over as he sat drinking that golden nectar, and with each day that passed he needed more to blot out the memories that surfaced. It was at this point he started to have an endless string of one night stands laced in cocaine, looking for that normalcy, and reassurance that he wasn't an animal after all, it was perfectly normal behaviour. His wife was just frigid. And then he was arrested.

Sitting in that rehab circle with other hopeless people, whom he found no connection with, some arrogantly refused to admit that they even had a problem. Unlike them he had not sold out his parents, or sold his body to buy things, he was not homeless. He wasn't poor or had come from a broken family he had a PHD and looked smart, unlike these losers. But he had to stay or face jail.

After the first forty eight hours the shakes convulsed in his body and he would have sold his soul for one tiny sip of whiskey, or a tiny line of white powder, just to take the edge off and after his fifth failed attempt at masturbating he found himself on the floor of his bathroom, defecated in his own vomit and faeces and then he cried for the first time in fifteen years. After catching a glimpse of his hollow, pallid, sweaty completion he knew that he was an addict. They said he had to go back to the root cause of his problems and to try and fix himself before he caused anyone or himself anymore pain. He knew that all of the answers were in the house.

A blanket of thick, grey clouds covered him as he struggled to move through them but he made it to the edge of the rickety bridge, which rippled with delight as each tyre began to move over it like he was on a conveyer belt forcing him in one direction. There was no going back. On the cliff edge he could see the waves galloping in force on each side then retreat then back with a force crashing into the rocks, spraying his car and penetrating the open window. The salt water left a layer of spit, which momentarily distorted his vision.

He needed a drink.

His mouth was dry and his throat almost called out in desperation for that golden liquid. He wanted to feel the slight burn slowly moving down his gullet and settling in the warm embrace of his stomach. His whole body began to shake but he had to gain control. He shook his head and got back in the game.

The causeway was foggy with moist, misty air that almost choked him. A feeling of fear swamped him. But he had to carry on this ghastly landscape. It was so overgrown it could not be driven through. He had to do the rest on foot.

The sky, stuck somewhere between night and day, clung all around him he was beginning to feel tired and faint but he could finally see the house deep in the distance. That overwhelming feeling of familiarity hit him hard and he knew he was coming home.

Approaching the dense pathway, a sudden jolt erected his body, like someone was watching him. But, he continued on it was as though his dread was pulling him into the house.

A huge black worn out door fame greeted him. He knew that this door held the houses secrets. His secrets. His past. His clammy hand shook as he reached out to turn the once shiny door knob. The door creaked open revealing a strong, mouldy, damp stench. It was the smell of a decaying house. Decaying flesh. Death.

He walked into the living room, his eyes darted looking for the light switch. It was out. He fumbled around looking for a candle to light. Suspiciously placed on the table with a match, he found a candle and without question he lit it. He walked with pace through the house, he was startled by a banging noise coming from upstairs.

He carefully made his way up the familiar, abandoned, staircase laced with dusty old paintings of his family and made his way down the dark, long corridor.

He stopped at the bedroom door. He was seven years old again. He knew at once why he was the way he was. He knew behind this particular door was all the answers.

His stomach churned at the thought of going through it and with a deep breath he reached out his hand to open the door...

MATHEW BRIDLE

When my children were going through their GSCEs I thought it would be a good idea to go to evening class and try one in English. Much to my surprise, I passed.

Seven years later I found myself applying for an MA in Creative Writing, much in part due to the video of Martin Goodman, the man responsible for creating the course. Were it not for his gentle character and passion for his subject I would have tried somewhere else and doubtless struggled to get through it.

The course was an inspiration in itself, giving birth to two novels, one of which I completed during the course, the other an early work in progress.

I have met, online, some fascinating characters who have journeyed, supported, and encouraged across the finish line. Without them I sculked away into the long dark …

Darkened Soul

One

I saw, in brief moments through the thick smoke, the fleet was gone, as was the beast. The warm crackle of fire brightened the cry of the dying. A wave washed over my legs, cooling the burn in my thigh. The next one washed higher, nearer my waist. I had to move or become another casualty. The sky was there as was the sun; at least I hoped they were. Forcing myself to sit, I just stared at the destruction - fifty ships. Men, women, whole families - lost.

My leg was stiff, every step an effort, exacerbated by the shifting sand and the push-pull of the ocean. My wound called for attention, a ragged flap hung on a flesh hinge. Endless salt and sand, I had to find fresh water before I dried out.

The beach gave way to a ridge of tall grass filling the air with its susurrous sound; soothing, a gentle welcome to a new land. I let my hands play among the tallest stems, the coarse stalks brushed the sand from my skin, pleasurable, were it to have ceased there. By the time I had passed through the barricade, I was cut and grazed. My blood speckled hands stung. Then I heard it: the drum. Dull at first, a single beat from the dark horizon I later realised was the endless forest.

The dead were there, watching - their eyes dark marbles of blood. My crew and my friends, all of them, head bowed listening for the next beat, and when it struck, they took a step as though they had no will.

Thud. The drum called my name. Gentle as lover's call. I felt her breath upon my cheek, and my pain ebbed. I stepped toward the forest and its dark embrace, feeling exposed, I sought shelter, thinking there must be a settlement nearby, perhaps a fishing village or trapper's hut.

Another beat, another step, and so the necromancer called the thralls.

There was a chill, not unpleasant, a caution on the skin. I shuddered, hesitating at the fringe where hope remained in view. I wanted to run. I truly did, I did not try. What was there to go back to? My Elenor was by my side though she no longer knew the living from the dead. She just walked on that bone splinter towing her foot. Pity was all I felt. The best emotion I could muster. She was dead, as were they all. One child carried a wooden horse in one hand, in the other the tattered remains of a cat, its pink tongue lolled out of its crushed skull, one eye reduced to a residue, the other staring into oblivion.

I dared a look to the sea - darkness and nothing more. The day, the sky, the ships - all gone beneath the shroud of branches. Forward was the only way. Forward to the drum.

By a stream I came upon a gathering of the dead. I knelt to slake my thirst, and as I drank of the cold crystal, one eye on the dead, I saw my ghost in the shallows; my hair was gone, my face dark, but then all was dark in this creeping twilight. The waters muddied; they were crossing over. Step by stumbling step, no thought, just a response to the beat. I edged past them with increasing haste, I looked at each one, their faces familiar yet erased in death.

The soft rustle of leaf litter gave way to the hard clump of bare earth, and there stood the drum bathed in torchlight. Taller than any man, too wide to wrap in my arms. The base rested on feet, skewered through the heel into the caked earth. The sides were bones, ground smooth. The skin was stretched so tight the veins cut pathways to its heart where a severed skeletal fist thumped its face.

Then I saw her. Angel or demon? I knew nor cared not. Her skin glowed in the torchlight, so pale, yet so alive. Her bosom was full, round, inviting my eyes to follow their curves to her waist, belly and legs. Her modesty covered by her snaking black hair. She was smiling. Those lips parted to speak, but I heard no sound, I felt what was said, and was smitten to serve.

'Eat,' she said. 'The table is laid. The meat is ready.'

There, on a table carved around the fattest oak lay a spread so delectable my stomach gurgled in anticipation of the succulent flesh. I feasted on breast, rump, belly, and thigh, all the meat I desired. So rich a table I had never known. A taste of heaven kissed my lips with every bite. I devoured it all, enthralled, a ravenous beast, nothing could compare. Sated, slumped across the offering, exhausted beyond resistance. I reached for a drink, dark and thick.

'What is your name, warrior?' Her tone harder than before, as audible as any.

'Barramon. I'm no warrior.' Her hand stayed the goblet from my mouth.

'Not yet, but soon you will wield power like no man in your land. I have seen it, so it shall be.'

'You are mistaken. I -'

'I am not mistaken, Barramon of Narelzbad. Your people fled the orcs after the Dark Star fell to the earth and birthed Doom's Rise.' She slid behind me drawing her fingers up my neck. 'I feel the mana rising in you.'

'I know nothing of what you speak,' I jumped to my feet pushing her aside. A soft wind breathed through the forest rippling her hair, such delights I had not thought of in many years. Elenor was the only woman I had known. And yet...

'You desire me.'

'I will not partake.' I did not see her move until her lips were upon my own. Her taste; rancid filth and decay. I shoved her aside. Her laughter was a chattering brook. 'What are you?' The strength of my voice startled me.

There, in the light of a small torch her face slipped. Someone else was trying to speak through her. 'Kill me!' a young woman vanished with a shriek.

'What is this?' I placed the goblet on the table and took up the knife, its long blade caked with old blood. Then I saw it; the remains of my meal. A body, its clothing torn from it. Chunks of flesh taken from the breast, buttocks and inner thigh. Teeth marks, everywhere as though she had been ravaged by savages. A foot tethered by a tendon, hung forlorn. I fell to my knees and howled, deep guttural anguish. What had I sunk to?

'Kill me!' her shriek yanked me back from the abyss. I leapt to my feet and sprang at her in feral fury. The knife sank into her belly, over and over as my teeth tore at her throat. She held on to me impassioned, her legs embraced me as I rode her to the ground cracking her spine on the firestone. Her arteries burst in my mouth, juicy as a summer berry.

Her legs slid down my sides, we were free. 'Seek me at the Cavern of Souls.' The wind took her words north, to where I did not know.

'Thank you,' Such gratitude for so violent an act! I rolled onto my back and stared at the tangle of branches. Fingers of sunlight stroked the earth. Morn or eve, I could tell, but their touch was a balm to my soul. Exhausted, sleep embraced me.

Two

Now the forest was alive. Timid chatter among the birds as though they had just learned to talk. Small creatures snouted through the leaf litter in search of grubs and worms. The musty woodland scent carried the taste of death. My crew lay all around, bodies broken and burned - peace for them at least.

Everything ached, my leg stung with every move, the wound filthy as the rest of me. Birds scattered from the trees in a squawking flurry as my scream rent the morning. A vile ooze surfaced from my injury as I staggered to the nearest support. Wiping the sleep from my eyes, I saw the shafts of the morning sun dance upon the stream. I fought back the pain, forced my limbs to carry me forth until I fell into the water and drank and drank until my mouth was clean of corrupt flesh. I retched and watched my vomit swirl away, wretch that I am, it amused me. Scooping up handfuls of the cold salve I scourged myself until my skin was raw.

I have no memory of my travail through the forest. How many trees were there? More than people? Less trouble too.

A broad river, with a voice of reeds bordered the forest. Pieces of deck, supply crates, fragments of life riding the flood tide toward mountains so grand they scoured the sky, rendering it a cloudless blue. I watched the debris float by. Some of the larger pieces gathered where a battered bridge hung like a scoop. The shoreline was smooth, worn smooth by the caress of endless tides. The bridge was narrow; its boards trailed green weed in wistful ribbons of mermaid's hair. The current pulled at my calves as the bridge sank under my weight, the flotsam scraped its bulk over the planks scarring the old timbers. I crossed over, glad to feel the earth beneath my feet

This land was a green field without beginning or end. Bees bumbled through the tall grass, shouldering their way to the honey-cup flowers whose golden bowls glinted in the sun. Branches hung in mighty thews tremulous with fists of blossom gloved in pink and blue, the scent so pungent it cleared my lungs in gasping blows. The clang of bells punctuated the bleating goats, whose concentric curled horns reminded me of the painted snails on the beaches back home. I remember the soft song of the sea when I held them to my ear, such enchantment I would never feel again.

'You look lost,' a voice gravelled.

'More than lost. I cannot see to whom I speak,' Sat among the gnarled roots, a fisherman, the pink palm of his hand a beacon against the black bark.

'Arrborn,' the white of his smile broke his face, illuminating the centre of his wild beard.

'What manner of man are you?'

'Do you not have dwarves where you come from?'

'We have orcs.'

'Come, sit, while I catch breakfast.' I watched him bait his hook with old fish guts; the stench was incredible, but he just whistled as he stabbed the hook through the squirming mess. 'Razor fish, go crazy for this.' His eyes burned with life, never have I seen such fire. The baited hook splattered on the water, a trail followed it down through the mirk. Instantly the line went tight jerking the dwarf from his roost. 'Here we go, matey.' His arms bulged with effort, filling the space in his tunic with taught muscle. 'Come to Arrborn, I only want to eat yer.' The line scythed through the water shredding the current. The dwarf, pulled against every change of direction, trying to turn the head of the fish. 'No, yer don't,' Arrborn leaned back pulling the fish from the depths. 'Get ready to - DUCK!' A green striped missile flew toward us its mouth a nest of nails. Arrborn leapt on it as it floundered on the earth, beating it with his fists until it lay still. 'He's a beauty, about the size of my mother. Do you mind?'

I picked up the fish in both hands to keep it from dragging on the ground and followed after the dwarf through some trees into a copse where a large house sat beside a half-filled barn. 'Well this, surprises me,' the house looked as though it belonged to someone much larger.

'You never know who's coming to tea,' he poked at the fish. 'Or breakfast.'

'Where do you want the fish?'

'Kitchen. This way,' Arrborn left the door open. The clatter and clank of pots assailed me as I entered the kitchen, the dwarf was already chopping onions into a dark iron skillet sat over coals. 'You never saw me do this,' the glint in his eye turned orange. Fire erupted from his fingers bringing the coals to heat. 'I'm not supposed to do that, but then again there are great many things I do which I am not supposed to.' He took the fish and tossed it on the table as though it weighed nothing. 'You've not seen magic, have you?'

I pulled the knife from my belt, 'May I?' I opened the fish's belly, one long slit, gill to tail.

'Separate the head for me will ya. It'll make a nice trophy for the wall.'

'So I see.'

Arrborn scooped the guts into his bait bucket and threw two fat fillets in the pan. The fish crackled and spat as he spread butter over it. 'What are those plates made of? I've not seen anything like them.' I held one in my hand, surprised at its lightness. I ran my fingers over the ridges, following the contours around the broad teardrop.

'Dragon scale,' Arrborn cast his gaze to the sizzling pan. 'We get them on the mountains to the North, The Dragon's Teeth. The whole place is full of them.' He fiddled with the fish, sprinkling salt and herbs over it, the toasting herbs masked the smell of the fish.

'North? That's where the voice said to go.'

'Voice?'

'I had a rough day, yesterday. My fleet was sunk by some beast. It came out of nowhere and wrecked all fifty ships. I am the only survivor.'

'I'm sorry. I just saw you come out of the forest and cross the bridge. Not many get out alive. In fact, you're the first.' He put the fish on two of the dragon scales and carried it outside where he set in on a table hewn from an old tree stump.

'You were saying - voice.'

'This is wonderful,' the fish melted in my mouth. I broke the flesh with my fingers and ate it with bread. There was a scented herbal drink, made from petals and honey, Elenor would have liked this. Ale would have been better.

'Did you see the witch?'

'Dead. That's when I heard the voice. Seek me at the Cavern of Souls.'

'Not a place for mortals,' his eyes were half-closed as he reached for the salt. 'Needs more.' He scattered salt across his meal as though seeding a field.

'My first day in this land, wherever I may be, has not been good. Unlike this - '

'The tea?'

'Tea? I like it,' I finished the dregs and set the cup back on the table. 'What's with the Cavern?'

'Full of dead things. Only the dead can go beyond the first gate. Providing, that is, you get past the guardians, they'll take a swing at anything.'

'You've been there?'

Arrborn swilled his drink in his cup, 'Just put a toe in, really. I've not the will for such a place. I'll show you where to go, if you're insistent on going.' We cleared the table and took the dishes back to the kitchen where we heaped them in a trough and pumped water over them. 'I'll get those later. This way.'

We went through the main room with its high-back chairs set in a crescent around a glowing hearth. The stairs wound around to the second floor opening out onto a broad landing where a desk sat covered in neat piles of parchment and scrolls.

'Did you draw all these?' The maps were extraordinary, such detail: every knoll and boulder, copse and dwelling, nothing was too insignificant.'

'Aye. I've a love of maps. Perhaps you could scribble one of your homeland, do a swap?' He tossed a scroll from one hand to the other and back again. 'That way no one loses, eh?'

'I can do that.' I waited for Arrborn to finish laying out the parchment and quills before I sat to create my memory of Narelzbad and the realms beyond its borders. 'Some of the towns will be gone by now. The orcs were razing everything that reminded them of us. Orcs were my friends once. The seer's son, Jourell, you'd have liked him. Had no interest in fighting. He loved papers, like you. He sought old prophecies, collected every scrap he could find and pieced them together.'

'You smile. you were close?'

'Doom's Rise. It's where the Dark Star fell. The whole of the rise is just the earth it spewed out. Nothing good has come from its intrusion.'

'Decapolis! Now that I've heard of. Huge city, covers the whole land, does it not?'

'It does.' I put the quill down and sat back. 'There, it's not much, but it's the best I can do. I don't have your flair.'

'No one does,' his laugh was infectious, he did it a lot, most anything would bring mirth to his black face.

He talked about Drakeshire, the land where my people died. Nothing good ever came out from there. He too, was glad the witch was dead, I never gave details, just the bare facts. If he wanted to know more, he could find the hag's hovel for himself.

'I'd be honoured if you'd rest for a night, get your strength back. If you intend to hunt out the cavern you'll need every crumb of strength you can get. You should have no bother crossing Mor, it's peaceful, mostly farmsteads. Belgor has a market tomorrow. I'll take you to it and set you on your way. I've no doubt we'll get a good mount there, too.'

'Here's a map,' Arrborn passed me a scroll from a pile beside a clay pipe. 'You smoke?' Taking the clay pipe from him I filled it with some tobacco from a pouch. With a click of his fingers he held a tiny fireball between his forefinger and thumb. He dropped it into the bowl of the pipe where it sank to the bottom and ignited the tobacco. Nothing tasted quite like it, a mixture of earth and flowers entwined with apple kissed with summer. Darkness covered my eyes, I was home, in Narelzbad. The soft scent of pine drifted on the breath of angels from the mountains. Long tailed wyverns played in the heights, gliding among the branches, their scales glittering in the sun. Children played on the needle carpet, orcs and humans together, my girl among them, her giggles a stream of rainbows colouring my memories - such memories.

When the light returned, I was back in the chair, the pipe empty but my tankard full. The sun peered over the lip of the windowsill with eyes of red and gold, beneath brows bruised by the encroaching night. A day had passed, and I cared not. Arrborn told tales, through delicate whorls of smoke, of misty mountains and flights of dragons. Fanciful accounts of wars between races I had never heard of; but was willing to learn from. His words flowed in rythmic notes, a philharmonic history of these strange lands. We drank, we smoked, we fellowshipped.

The mage wars had taken his father, who was a priest, as was he, they trained in some distant temple in a land called Grimlaw, the home of his people. He spoke of friends and I of family, he of battles and I of love - lamentations, all of it. The Dark Star had fallen, and the people took on its taint. Bitterness, anger - hatred, such things we had not known. Then… Accuson. Arrborn's face paled at the name, I thought he was intoxicated. When at last he spoke it was from the grave, as though he had become a mere mouthpiece for something - someone far greater. I had never felt so afeared, my skin prickled. I wanted to hide, to run from the terror of it, but instinct said it would find me anywhere. If I sank to the depths of the ocean it could drink it and reveal my shame.

Night took the stage accompanied by twinkling stars and chirping fireflies, 'They remind me of the ones back home, that sound, it's happiness and hope in a note.'

'Aye,' the dwarf slipped from his chair to the floor where he snored for the night. I went in search of a bed and found one to my liking. I slept a fitful sleep filled with dreams of the dark-haired mistress, the embodiment of pleasure. She called to me. I answered. She knew my name and what I had done, still she wanted me. I walked into her arms, felt her nakedness upon mine, those black wings wrapped around me as she drank of my soul leaving me a husk of a man.

BLANCHE

Now the sun was rising. There would be four hours before it set again. Blanche watched the sun paint the sky with orange and yellow while steam rose from the ground in aquatic snorts. The nascence of wind made the day feel warm though it would never get above freezing.

Route 1 was out of sight. They were in a depression nestled among the crags. She pulled the collar of her grey parka over her mouth, savouring the heat of her breath on her face. The ice-crusted snow fractured beneath her feet as she walked around the car to open the passenger door where her husband sat in a pathetic huddle. Reaching in, she unfastened his coat and lifted him out of the seat. A tiny gasp left his throat as the pure Icelandic air sterilised his lungs. 'Not long now, Jeremy.' Blanche turned toward the snow-striped mountain, the black volcanic rock showing through where the wind had stripped its bones.

Jeremy groaned as she carried him over the frozen ground, where hot springs could appear at any time, the land here was forever moving as the millstones of the earth, the tectonic plates of America and Europe ground together. Pillows of snow cuddled craters disguising bottomless pits where lava once flowed in thermic tides to the sea forming new land, where, eventually life would come, small, almost insignificant but life nonetheless.

'I'm sorry, my love, but this is best for both of us.' Sensing his frail shudder, she pulled him to her bosom. 'Do you remember our honeymoon, the laughter, the promises; the love we had? Our first day out from

Reykjavik. We went to Okjokull, the glacier, I thought of taking you there, but it too has gone. So I brought you here. To nowhere. The sun is almost up now, another half hour, and it will hit its height, and then it will sink and be gone.'

There is a saying in Iceland, 'If you don't like the weather, wait five minutes, and it will be different.' Those five minutes were up.

Blanche cowered from the sudden wind yanking at her hood, wisps of white hair trailed out from her woolly hat. One layer was not enough to keep out the probing arctic fingers. Cradling her husband in her arms, she forged ahead, sliding her feet across the ice and snow. The wind tugged his arms, ribbons of flesh parcelling tired bones. She paused to kiss Jeremy's blue lips as ice crystals stung her face fusing with her tears. She fell to her knees and wept as she lay his body in the snow. 'MND - Motor Neurone Disease,' that's what the specialist had said, three letters that drained their lives. They were looking forward to retirement and resting in each other's arms, watching the sun go down. There were no children. Barren. Fertile as the basalt of Hellisheidi, sitting pretty beneath the pink sky.

Blanche drew herself to her feet. Took up her cargo and walked toward the steam. The land beneath her creaked and groaned as she picked her way among the crevices until she found what she was looking for: a crater, not too wide, with a breath of steam, orange lipped. 'Your favourite colour,' forcing a smile, she lowered the withered husk of her love into the ground. A hush swept over the world, the only sound a soft mourning sob.

The wind gasped and was gone. Silence. Just the thud of tears falling in the snow. Through bleary eyes, Blanche watched as the land was brushed with yellow, orange, red as deep as her lips until the sun melted into the horizon snuffing out the light. Nothing left in the darkness except memories of a man whose strength carried her over the threshold, soothed the pain of miscarriage, and abated the fear of cancer with love so pure it kept no account of wrongs.

MIKE MCMASTER

Mike has worn many hats in his life (manager, lifeguard, radio DJ, church worker, husband and cat's minion) but is still trying to work up the nerve to put on the one that says "Writer". The Hull Creative Writing MA is a big step in that direction and the encouragement and support of teaching staff and the cohort of students is what carried him through the challenges and variety of the two years' study. His highly supportive wife and family may also have had something to do with it.

Whilst looking at MA options Mike realised that each course had at least one module that was not really his "thing". In most, it was poetry. At Hull, it was "Writing from Life" – for Mike the toughest module and, perhaps because of this, the one where he learned the most. It is no coincidence that he chose Southside Stories for this anthology – creative non-fiction, set in his beloved Birmingham.

Decisions was also an assessed piece for the course, and was long-listed by Cranked Anvil (www.crankedanvil.co.uk) in November 2020. It joins several other of Mike's pieces from the MA which have found a wider audience: Help Me (www.ripplesinspace.com), Cold and Coffee with Steve (www.365tomorrows.com) and Schrodinger's Café which was Short-listed by Furious Fiction in August 2019 (www.writerscentre.com.au/furious-fiction/).

As well as widening his reading range, developing new skills and introducing him to a wonderful gang of students, the course forced him to plan an entire novel and write the first chapter. He supposes he'd probably better finish it at some point. Mike is on Twitter at @MikeBham

DECISION

Two men in a room, deciding who is going to die, as they do every Wednesday. It should be an impossible choice but they measure out the value of a life with clinical precision. In moments.

The room smells of hospital cleaning products and over-tired junior doctors. David is one of them. His Professor paces the room with his watch-chain glinting as it catches the light. David is still and thoughtful.

"Well, doctor?" snaps the Professor. "Your recommendation?"

David pauses before he speaks. There is no over-dramatic wrinkling of his brow in thought or anxious wringing of hands, but his blue-grey eyes do seem a little harder, his shoulder are perhaps a fraction of an inch lower. His hand slips unseen below the table and seeks out his white coat pocket, fingers curling comfortingly around the bowl of his pipe.

Looking past the Professor, through the hospital window, David sees a jet starting its climb away from nearby Heathrow airport.

How does he weigh one life against another? How is he supposed to choose between patients? For one an opportunity for dialysis and for the other not even that slim hope, probably gone by the end of the week.

"Come on!" The watch-chain sparkles as it whirls around the room. "You know the protocol. Medical.

Social. Compliance. So, get on with it! Which patient is the highest priority?"

Who the patients actually are, their lives, professions, children, all this should be irrelevant. But David is their doctor and he has met families and made reassuring noises to spouses. He knows which patient is a mother who volunteers at a local soup kitchen, and which one is older, divorced and an ex-alcoholic who drank himself into the hospital bed.

Playing for time, David pulls out his pipe. His hands work automatically to trace the ritual of tobacco and lighter. The mother? The flame catches, the bowl crackles and the first mouthful of smoke is sweet. The ex-drinker? A few puffs buy another moment to think.

The watch-chain glints urgently through the haze of tobacco. Beyond, the jet is already out of sight, lost in the low clouds.

"Well sir," David voice is still, calm and thoughtful. "I have assessed both patients and I do have a recommendation."

Walking onto the renal ward, past the Nurses' Station, David catches a little of their conversation as they hand over between shifts.

"…so I'm in checking Seven. Urine output. And he tries to grab my bum. That's the second time today. Nasty piece of work if you ask me, and very handsy, so just make sure you…"

The advice is lost as David moves onto the ward. Bay Seven is at the far end, and whilst "nasty piece of work" is not a formal medical description, it seems pretty appropriate to David. The nurses have been complaining about this patient ever since he was referred to the unit, matching the complaints streaming from the patient himself. Food, medication, noise, temperature, nurses, doctors – everything draws criticism and contempt. He's the only patient on the unit referred to by his number. No-one wants to know his name.

The curtains are drawn around Bay Seven, and David can hear voices chattering softly on the other side. He pauses. The illusion of privacy that this flimsy sheet of wipe-clean fabric offers is absolute on the ward. Patients cling to this lie, otherwise the reality of enduring the day-to-day necessities of life – bed pan, catheter, enema – within a few feet of strangers overhearing every intimate noise, that would be too much. David is always impressed at how hard a patient will grasp at dignity, even when everything else is falling away.

Bay Seven is not used to quiet conversations. This is the first visitor David has seen since the patient arrived. He gives them another moment.

The voices pick up, there is a cheerful "Bye then!" and the curtain is flicked aside by a blond streak of energy and enthusiasm. A boy, brown and orange striped shirt, short trousers and untied shoelaces skips out of the bay and dances off down the ward, smiling and waving at the nurses.

Stepping into the bay, David finds Seven sitting up in bed, with a smile fading. Just for a moment David catches a glimpse of what this man could be like when he wasn't being prodded, drugged, and scrutinised. When he wasn't afraid. Then the smile is gone, and the hard, accusing stare is back.

"Well? What do you want?"

"Ah, I wanted to have a chat about your treatment. But your visitor, er, I didn't know that you had a…grandson?"

"I haven't. He's her boy. Lady in the bed down the ward." Seven pauses and looks down at his lap, where a yellow toy truck nestles, fragile and bright against his puffy hands. "He's a good kid."

"Indeed. Perhaps we could talk about your situation for a moment. You were referred to us by your Hepatic Physician because your longer-term liver issues are impairing your kidneys. Our assessment puts you at about 6% of normal kidney function, and that is declining."

"Yeah, yeah. Swollen legs, short of breath and I can't piss any more. Get on with it."

"Well, we have reviewed your case as part of our process of determining priorities for treatment. As you know, we have limited capacity on the unit for kidney dialysis."

Seven raises his chin and looks directly at David.

"And I'm not priority? No surprise there. 'Brought it on himself' they say. 'His own fault'."

"No, that's not what…"

"Bollocks. I've heard the whispers. I know what people think. Maybe they're right. Maybe I did drink myself into this mess, but let me tell you. I haven't touched a drop in two years. Not since the doctor told me. I've been to every appointment, swallowed every damn tablet, taken every single test, scan and stabbing that you bastards have thrown at me, and I cannot believe after all that you are just going to give up. Fuck. You."

"That's enough. We are not interested in whispers. We make our decisions based on evidence. Medically, your liver issues have stabilised and the prognosis there is quite good, so we need to get on top of the renal problems. Social – no family, but also nothing that might impede the treatment. And Compliance. You are quite right – for twenty-four months you complied with everything demanded of you. So, stop swearing at me. You are scheduled to start dialysis tomorrow."

At this point, patients are usually relieved, effusive in their thanks or just tearful and smiling. But David watches as Seven lowers his gaze and slowly turns the toy truck over and over in his hands. When Seven speaks, his voice is much softer.

"What about the lady down the ward?"

David's response is automatic. "I cannot discuss the details of another patient with you."

"What's going to happen to her? The kid says she's really sick. 4% or something. Is she on the list too?

"I cannot discuss that. But there was only one slot open for a new dialysis patient this week."

The toy truck turns over and over, and then stops.

"Would you kindly explain what the hell happened." The Professor's irritation isn't hiding behind professional propriety.

"He declined the treatment." David finds maintaining his normal calm exterior harder than he expected. The last time they were in this room they were taking the impossible decisions, but now it is somehow more difficult to report the extraordinary choice made by the patient himself.

"Declined? And why in God's name did he do that? Does he understand the consequences?"

"He understands very well, sir. We had a long chat, but he would not change his mind. I did persuade him to agree to go onto the transplant list, but with his declining function, he'd need a new kidney in the next few days, and what are the chances of a donor in that time?"

The Professor stares out of the window in frustration, his watch-chain reflecting in the pane of glass as the skies beyond darken.

"Hmph. Well, maybe he'll get away with it. There's always some reckless twenty-year old out there with a new motorbike and a death wish."

The watch-chain whirls as the professor turns round and claps David on the shoulder.

"Cheer up doctor, it looks like rain. That should bring in a donor or two before the weekend!"

SOUTHSIDE STORIES

Half way down Hurst Street a large, silver, sparkling rhinoceros overlooks the crossroads, marking a boundary. Behind us are the sour sweet smells of the Chinatown restaurants, the crowded pavements outside the Hippodrome Theatre as the evening show ends and the endless stream of taxis disgorging giggling, glammed-to-the-max girls and tough shabby-immaculate boys. They all head for the bars and nightclubs, hunting for the cheapest drinks, loudest music and each other.

The Rhinestone Rhino stands at the northern edge of the Gay Village. From where it perches, two storeys up, it has an unrivalled view of the whole length of arrow-straight Hurst Street. The statue's mirrored hide reflects a thousand glimpses of the community at its feet.

A rhinoceros was first used in gay rights campaigning in Boston in 1974. Daniel Thaxton and Bernie Toale, two Boston artists with Gay Media Action, planned a public advertising campaign for March, to raise the profile of the LGBT community in Boston. They selected a purple rhinoceros as the symbol because, according to Toale, "it is a much maligned and misunderstood animal" – shy, gentle and intelligent. The colour was a mix of pink and blue, a blending of masculine and feminine.

The quirky poster advertising campaign attracted more attention than the artists anticipated. Metro Transit Advertising, who initially approved the advertisements' designs, raised the display charge from $2 to $7 per site. This was beyond the budget of Gay Media Action, who cancelled the campaign and took legal action instead. The transit authority stood by their decision to raise the charges, but the resultant publicity launched the campaign into the public awareness, and a large papier-mâché Lavender Rhino appeared at the Boston Pride march. Badges, T-shirts and banners all displayed the rhinoceros symbol.

Gay Media Action received enough donations to run a reduced-scale poster campaign of 100 sites on the metro for 3 months, ending in February 1975. The rhino's influence lived on. Adopted by the LGBT community it appeared in further Pride marches. A decade later the small awareness campaign had created a powerful international symbol, and was celebrated on a flag raised over Boston City Hall in 1987.

Steve and I are on patrol. We walk the length of Hurst Street stopping to talk to the door staff at the pre-club bars, the private party venues and the strip clubs. We chat with the promoters in their skimpy costumes, towering stilt walkers, paraffin-perfumed fire-breathers and dancers, waxed and oiled to a shine. We say hello and smile to everyone who walks past. Some smile back. Some stop and stare. In this midnight sea of rainbows, tattoos and piercings our appearance is strange; two middle-aged men in black and white jackets, carrying shoulder bags full of water, flip flops, plasters, tissues, hand sanitiser and oh-so-many plastic bags.

The street is, as usual, marred by abandoned bottles. This one, that my foot has just nudged, is still rolling gently in the gutter, the wet glass reflecting street-lights in a glistening sheen. I don't need to bend down to recognise the shape, the cheap thin glass and the gaudy label – Lambrini.

This bottle rode here in one of those taxis crammed with excited girls pre-loading for their night out. Cheap wine on the back seat is far more cost effective than the huge prices inside the nightclubs. The multiple shades of lipstick smeared on the bottle's neck show that it was passed round the group, eager swigs mixing with giggles and the obligatory selfies. The taxi-driver reminding them of the extra charges if they make a mess. One girl perhaps quieter in the corner as she worries about running into her ex. And there is always one who is louder, brash and full of vodka-inspired confidence. She'll be the one vomiting and incoherent in a doorway by midnight.

My fingers anticipate the sticky surface as I reach for the bottle. A couple of inches of colourful, sugar-saturated liquid lurk at the bottom. Just how desperate would you need to be to swig such dregs? I've seen it happen – the dirty and discarded street-people pick through the dropped party-bottles and drain each one for any last trace of alcohol. Not this bottle – I upend it, pour out the syrupy booze and put the empty bottle in the bin. This one won't feed any more addictions, or be snatched up in a drunken rage and weaponised.

Our radio crackles. I twist the volume to hear over the sounds crashing out of the bar behind us.

"Brum Pastors. Arcadian Security. Are you receiving?"

"Arcadian Security. This is Brum Pastors. Go ahead."

"Pastors, please attend at the Iris Hotel. Door staff have requested assistance with an uncooperative guest."

"Received. On our way."

The uncooperative guest is outside the hotel when we arrive, hammering on the glass door.

"Fucking let me in!"

She is wearing a sheer black dress, cut so low at the front and so short at the hem that a significant amount of very cold skin is visible. Her clutch-bag is on the ground at her feet, next to one of her high heels. She is still wearing the other one, her stance lopsided and unstable. Her slurring and swaying tells us this is not just because of the shoes.

"Need to get in. Open the door."

She swings another punch at the glass. The movement twists her foot off her shoe. She slumps sideways. Steve is fast and catches her. We ease her down to sit on the pavement. Her arms are cold to the touch.

"Hello. I'm Steve and this is Mike. We are Brum Pastors. Can we help you at all?"

"Just want to get indoors. Fuckers won't let me in."

"Let's see if we can help you. You look cold."

Steve starts to unwrap one of our foil blankets. I move over to the door and nod to the security guard inside. He slides the door open a few inches.

"So, what's the story?"

"She was in our lobby, shouting at the guests and falling over everywhere. We tried to help but you can see what state she's in."

"Perhaps we can help get her up to her room?"

The guard frowns.

"Room? She's not a guest here. She's not got a room or a reservation."

Steve has the foil blanket wrapped round her. He is chatting away as I squat down next to them.

"She says her name is Sarah."

"Hello Sarah. I've had a chat with the hotel and they say that you are not booked in with them. So, what's going on?"

Her head lolls round and she looks at me for a moment.

"Want to go home."

"Well, I think that is probably a good idea. Do you want us to call someone?"

"Can't."

She fumbles in her clutch-bag and drops a mobile phone on the ground. The phone case is all glitter and sparkles and a cute "Hello Kitty" logo. The screen is blank.

"Battery's dead."

"OK. Maybe we could call someone for you on one of our phones?"

"Want to go home. Phone Mum."

"Do you know her number?"

"In my phone."

"I see. Well, is there anyone else we could call? Did you come out with friends, tonight?"

"Not friends. People from work."

"OK, maybe we can find them. Where do you work?"

"School. St Mary's." She raises her head and straightens up a little. "I'm a teacher."

Storm sits on his torn cardboard mat, hunched over a wrecked plastic bottle. His growl is the low rumble of a diesel truck and his whole body vibrates as his lips peel back to reveal huge yellow teeth. I extend my hand very slowly for him to administer the customary sniff of identification. The snarl subsides and his tail, a snubbed and scraggy stump, twitches. Storm knows that smell. It is usually followed by something tasty.

Encountering Rich, Storm's owner, is a similar process. We are careful to avoid walking up behind him and instead take a detour to approach from in front. In appearance, Rich is quite a contrast to his dog. Most of his teeth are missing, and Storm's shiny coat is significantly cleaner than the mass of stains, rags, patches and filth that cloaks Rich. Then there is the street-dirt smell; urine, vomit, stale sweat, congealed grease stains and cigarette-ends cut through with his breath. A decade of halitosis mixed with the sweet tang of high strength cider.

Rich looks up, grins at us and holds out his dirt-crusted hand for me to shake. Tonight, he's in a good mood. Which means he's had a drink, and has probably made up with his partner, Sarah. For now.

Gav is lurking in his doorway. His dark suit is stretched over his huge muscles and his black shirt has several buttons open as no collar is going to easily fit round his neck. Tattoo flames writhe up from inside the shirt and climb almost to his face before vanishing into his beard – the only hair on his shaved head. His hands are immense. Chunky gold rings adorn most fingers, giving Gav permanent knuckle-dusters in the guise of jewellery. He is rejecting a hopeful customer as we walk up.

"Didn't like the look of 'im", Gav explains.

I have never seen Gav let anyone into the lap-dancing club that he guards. Cerberus in a black suit, he turns away drunk teenagers, furtive businessmen and stag do's with the same menacing growl. Then a dancer steps out of the club, scanty garments half-covered with a bathrobe in an attempt at warmth. She's grabbing a cigarette between clients, and Gav is suddenly all smiles, courtesy and charm as he flips out a lighter.

The cigarette is gone in thee long drags. She disappears back into the darkness of the club before her goosebumps turn to shivers in the frosty night.

"My brother's gonna look after my dog this week."

Gav's announcement catches me by surprise, and I take a moment to work out the significance.

"Er ... is that because of the court case?" I hazard.

"Yeah. Court ain't no problem though. Nothing to it. Piece of piss."

"So, you are feeling confident about it?"

"Totally. In the end it is just her word against mine. And she's lied about so much stuff already, no one is going to believe her. I mean. Sending threats by text. Would I really be that stupid? Whole thing will get thrown out, no worries."

This is normal for Gav. His confidence is his shield. In his stories he is always in the right, the police have never got a clue what they are doing and everyone else is always lying or trying to set him up. In the eighteen months that we have been meeting him we've never seen even the faintest crack in that armour.

Steve picks up the conversation. "Your brother is going to look after your dog, is he?"

"Yeah. For a few days, like. Just in case, you know."

"Just in case?"

The finest hairline crack. Steve gently taps at the armour.

"Just in case the court hearing doesn't go the way you expect?"

"Well…yeah."

"Hmm. How do you feel about that?"

"Yeah…no good…not too good really."

Gav pauses. His hands are fumbling with one of his larger rings, and his eyes are looking down, away, anywhere but at Steve.

"I mean…well…it should be alright but…you never know…" He turns his face towards us slowly. "It might all go tits up and then…"

"That must be very worrying."

"Yeah. Yeah. Worrying. Yeah."

"Frightening?"

"Well…yeah."

Gav looks like a lost child. Steve reaches out and puts a hand on his shoulder.

"Would you like us to pray for you about it?"

There is a long pause.

"Yeah. Yeah. That would be good."

We stand in the strip-club doorway and, heads bowed, pray for the powerful, frightened, violent, lonely doorman.

The Rhinestone Rhino, gender neutral and covered in pieces of smashed mirrors and fake diamonds, shines from its rooftop perch as an intentionally fabulous marker of the northern edge of Birmingham's Gay Village. It was craned onto its plinth in 2012 and is an accurate, life-sized sculpture of a Black Rhinoceros (Diceros bicornis). With extra sparkle.

Three Scotland-based artists, Emma Butler, Vikki Litton and Robbie Coleman, were commissioned to create the sculpture. Working over five months they carved polystyrene and covered it with fiberglass and mirror fragments, held on with industrial-strength swimming pool adhesive grout.

Beneath the acrylic gemstones the rhino contains a secret. Conceptual artist Jo Hodges gave the rhino a heart, nestled deep inside the sculpture. The heart holds stories and photographs. The rhino is the guardian of the thoughts, feelings and memories of Birmingham's gay and lesbian communities. The gemstones hark back to Birmingham's jewellery-making heritage.

It was unveiled at the start of the Birmingham Pride festival. When it was illuminated, it radiated cascades of light over the crossroads. A glamourous glitterball transforming the street below into a glorious disco. It even had its own (unofficial) Twitter account for a few years, promoting the bars and clubs of the gay district.

Walking beneath the Rhinestone Rhino, Steve and I almost pass a man lying, face hidden, against the wall. We usually chat with the homeless but we are careful not to disturb them when they are sleeping. This chap, though...something doesn't seem right. We slow down. His shoes are smart, black and shiny. His clothes are a suit, quite clean, and he has a bulky gold chain around his wrist. This isn't the normal attire for a street-person. I kneel down next to him.

"Hello. Hello? We're Brum Pastors. Are you alright?"

No response.

I lean in and see that there is something on the back of his head, concealed in his tangled, curly black hair. My torch beam reveals a dark, sticky mass of congealing blood, and more pooled on the pavement beneath him.

"Hello? Hello? Can you hear me? Are you OK?"

No response.

ABC. Airway. Breathing. Circulation. It is a frosty night, so I hold my mobile phone right up against his face. A faint trace of breath condenses on the screen. Glove off, I can feel a weak pulse in his neck. I unwrap a clean micropore gauze bandage and apply it to the wound, covering the deep gash. I sit carefully cradling the man's head. Steve spreads a foil blanket over him, then steps back to assess the situation.

"Excuse me, do you know this man? Excuse me, did anyone see what happened?"

The passers-by continue to pass by. No-one is very interested in hanging around on a cold night. Some people see us and cross the road to keep clear.

Steve takes a decision, and thumbs his radio.

"Arcadian Security, this is Brum Pastors. Are you receiving?"

"Receiving. Over."

"Arcadian, we have an IC3 male, unconscious and with a head injury, on the pavement outside the Hurst Street Car Park. Do you have us on camera?"

"Stand by."

Half a mile away in the Control Room the security operator switches between the dozens of cameras at his command. He zooms in on us, our distinctive black and white jackets easy to spot on screen.

"Brum Pastors, Security. Yes, I can see you. Do you need help?"

I nod to Steve. The man is still unconscious and his face is cold to the touch. I'm really worried about him.

"Arcadian Security, yes please. Could we have an ambulance? Quickly, please."

"Stand by."

We stand by. Steve stays on his feet, making sure that no-one decides to get involved. Drunken clubbers often mean well but inebriated assistance is far more of a hinderance than help. I stay sitting on the pavement, checking pulse and breathing. I talk to the man. As he remains unconscious it is a pretty one-sided conversation, but I remember something from a First Aid Course about people hearing far more than we think, so I keep up a gentle chatter of reassurance.

"Hello. I'm Mike. I'm a Brum Pastor. Don't worry, we going to look after you. How are you feeling? Looks like you've had a bit of a bump on the head. We'll get that sorted out. We've got an ambulance on the way, and they will take care of you. Do you remember what happened? Not to worry, I am sure we can sort it all out. You look like you've dressed up for the evening. Have you been out with friends? Or maybe you were at the theatre earlier. Was it a good show?"

No response.

It is a long, cold quarter of an hour before the ambulance arrives with a swirl of blue lights, green paramedic jumpsuits and white latex gloves. The professionals take over and we step back. The man, still unresponsive, is lifted onto a stretcher and loaded into the ambulance. More blue lights and they are gone, leaving a dark sticky pool congealing on the pavement, and a ripped foil blanket flapping gently in the breeze.

"I nearly walked past him", I admit to Steve. "I thought he was just drunk."

"So did I, mate."

Two men, young, sun-tanned and stylish dressers, are taking turns to lean against the Hurst Street road-sign. They are using a camera as well as their mobile phones to take pictures, posing with the street sign, pointing, smiling. One of them squats down and hugs the sign.

"We're on holiday!" the man currently holding the camera explains.

"Yes, yes," his friend joins in. "Please, take the photograph of us."

We oblige. They are delighted to be in a picture together.

"Where are you from?"

"Nice in France. Do you know it? It is much warmer than Birmingham! But we had to come here."

"Yes, we had to come. We have been to Abbey Road. I'll show you."

The mobile screen blurs as pictures scroll past. There they are, posing on a zebra crossing.

"We love The Beatles."

"So I can see." I'm intrigued. Not by Abbey Road, but this is the first time I've heard of a Birmingham street being on the tourist trail.

"So, why did you come here?"

"This is Hurst Street. So famous. So important. You have the Pride here. Every summer. We have seen the Pride and we had to come to visit the clubs."

"And see the street," his friend chips in. "Please, a few more pictures?"

Near The Nightingale, the oldest gay nightclub in Birmingham, our smiled "hello" is thrown back at us in a spray of saliva.

"Fuck off!" The young man, black sleeveless Tee and a cross on a chain round his neck, shouts at us. "Fuck off! This is our space. You don't belong here."

"What happened?" asks Steve. "Who hurt you?"

The effect is instantaneous. The young man's anger switches off, pain is all over his face, in his voice, pushing tears down his cheeks.

"Not me. I don't give a fuck what they think about me. Fucking church."

He's sobbing now, the words struggling out between huge gasps that shake his thin body. Steve steps closer.

"Tell us what happened."

"I don't care that they kicked me out. Expected it. But..."

He stops.

We sit on the pavement together. I fish clean tissues from my bag and pass them to him. He starts twisting them in his hands.

"They didn't have to do that to my Mum! They made her choose. Me or the church. My Mum! She'd been to mass every Sunday since forever. How's she supposed to choose between that and her family?"

Steve voice is soft now. "I am so sorry. I am so sorry for all the pain and hurt that has been caused to you and to your mother."

We are all crying as Steve puts an arm round his shoulders to hug him.

Gay Media Action chose the rhinoceros as their symbol. Often misunderstood due to its appearance, it is a strong, docile and intelligent creature, but if it is angered or threatened, it fights. Ferociously.

ZHARKO ZACH BLIZNAKOV

Zharko Zach Bliznakov is a Writer and an English lecturer at South China University of Technology. He has a BA Hon degree in English Language and Literature and an MA in English Creative Writing.

Zach's strength is his perseverance and inability to quit until a particular skill is learned, a job is done, or a goal is accomplished. His students are often surprised at the high standards he holds them to but feel secure in the knowledge that he is their most loyal supporter, as he provides encouragement and guidance to ensure they reach their full potential.

When he's not attending to his full schedule, you can find him and his dog, Ryan, on a long hike in the mountains trekking through rough terrain no matter the weather. His love of exploring and photography is not only confined to nature; every six months, Zach explores a different country and learns different culture, food, and people. The architecture of big cities and empty streets at night are as exciting as people watching in packed rowdy bars in peak hours. Zach can often be spotted at a window table with his notebook and pen or a good novel set in the country he's currently travelling in.

THE RELUCTANT STORYTELLER

I knew I could have stopped you. You gave me several opportunities: the sobbing, the slamming of cupboard doors and the exaggerated banging of the chest of draws. I was not callous, or worse, indifferent. It was not a disregard for the years we spent together, it really wasn't. I could've stopped you when you said in the most exasperated of voices, barely audible: I cannot do this anymore, Janick. I just can't.

I heard you packing, I could've said, please stop. I could have rushed to the landing when I heard you drag the suitcase and shove it down the stairs. You waited, you hesitated at the front door, even after you buttoned up your coat and pulled on your boots. I had the opportunity to go into the hallway and plead with you. I have done it so many times before, I know you have this deep compassion and understanding. I could have come clean then, right there with the Uber driver waiting in a snowfall. Don't think for a minute that it didn't cross my mind. And a part of me wanted to hold you, brush the stray dark curls off your forehead and tell you that it's all my fault. All of this is on me. All of it.

I watched as the dark blue Honda disappeared down the white landscape, white smoke puffing from the exhaust. I don't know if you looked back, it was too dark to see. I know the silence you left is still filling the room and settling on my desk. The silence is on every blank page terrorizing me in soft candle light. I really want to tell this story; I've been wanting too for so long. I don't know if the story is mine to tell, maybe it belongs to Goran, maybe it's Goran's story? In the dark silence the characters appear and disappear in my mind, half formed, taunting, mocking on spring mornings, in fragrant blossoms or urgent water rushing downstream and you, always you, your face so white and eyes opaque. I did love you and maybe all of that love is still here somewhere. As I said, this is on me.

You stayed in the hotel room in Rome on the day I went for the tour at the Vatican. You were upset, you said it was supposed to be romantic, it was supposed to fix all that was dysfunctional in the marriage. You made an effort; please don't think I didn't notice. You looked beautiful in the silvery grey negligee. I wanted to, I too had so many hopes pinned on that break. I know you said you adored me despite the weight I had gained. You said it didn't matter to you, you loved me.

I just didn't love myself. I couldn't find a love big enough in me to love what I've become. And then he was there on the majestic staircase at the museum, I heard his voice and the very first time I heard the most beautiful word I have ever heard: Meliora. It was the voice I recognized. A distinct, clear voice with Slavic tones: 'Meliora is probably the most beautiful Latin word, don't you think? I turned and we both took a few steps back. The shock on your face was visible and I'm felt the blood drain from mine. But the frisson was still there, right there on the steps of the Vatican Museum, witnessed by God, you said that later.

Goran, Goran Jelinik, meliora; to improve, the words mull in the falling snow. I settle with a glass of merlot and watch as the night covered the blanketed snow in the front yard.

Where to go with all these memories and the unrequited self-love?

Dear reader, I don't know if you've ever lost someone in a divorce? I don't know if a lover has ever walked away from you, or maybe you're the one that left? If so, you'll know exactly what I'm talking about. A silence descends and it's so easy to mistake this silence for peace. Those few minutes when you think peace has finally arrived, terror comes out of nowhere, like an animal trying to find a gap in a fence, you try and re-engineer a future previously unimagined, not yet designed.

You see, you were too busy fighting, too busy blaming and too busy looking back, and now there's a terrifying new future with only you and all your failings to redesign.

And even if you have someone new to go to, you have all your shortcomings to take with you into the new future. Your failures and your areas of lack were just highlighted, magnified in the split from someone who once adored you. Their scent still in every corner of the house.

Jo Malone's Pomegranate Noir was still in the air, on the pillows, the signature morning fragrance when the smell of fresh coffee and your scent waltzed around the edges of our living spaces. It will fade through the week. It will be replaced by my stale cigarette smoke. I know, I don't smoke, but I've taken up the old habit during the battle. Slowly, my slovenly ways will result in a rancid odour permeating the dusty corners of the deathly quiet house.

I know it sounds depressing, and believe me, it was. I don't know if it is the sheer amount of time I spent denying who I am, duelling with God, thinking I really love you, Elena, and then hating the things you said and who both of us became toward the end.

It sounds very self-indulgent, I know, but it is a time when you are solely focused on yourself and your feelings and trying to make sense of it all. You can self-sooth or self-medicate — and those to become your only choices. Anyway, I seem to be in the middle of building a museum of memories, and the room where I'm currently at is that of horror. Everything I try and write seems wrong, infantile whining from a grown man.

I sip from the glass, savouring the peppery berry notes and watch the snow. Always the snow with you and I, wherever we went the winter was always there. Long, harsh, cold winters that only Eastern Europe can deliver. I put another log on the fire and watch the flames burn through the papers I toss in, consuming fragments of our past, turning it to ash in the grid.

Fire and snow, The Freezing Fire, I thought might be a good title for our story. Even on our first date: you wanted to hang out at Kulušić, Saloon was the place to be seen and God knows, you were so cool I wanted to follow you, to be part of your punk rock world. Not that I wasn't already part of the scene. I was a writer at Polet, a struggling one for sure, but Polet was the new hipster magazine and I wanted to write about the evenings you inhabited, you with your impossibly dark, long curls and opaque eyes like onyx disks set in kohl with long lashes catching tears as they fell. But that came later.

The night we hopped on the old mustard tram to cross the Sava. Its waters dark and calm. My forensic examination of every part of you: your dark velvet hat with the huge fake safety pin, a nod to the punk scene, the black coat with its turned-up collar. It was only September and snow fell on Sljeme Square. We entered the Saloon. The Clash was de rigueur back then. I think it is I'm so Bored With the U.S.A. and White Riot that I remember from that night. We drank Cézar, a brandy that flowed through hipster veins at the time. People were dancing and we talked like lovers do in the first flush of infatuation, when we found ourselves and our stories so fascinating that we wanted to share and over-share. You told me about your childhood, your alcoholic father, and your submissive mother, how you would never be in that situation. Your life was about freedom, you were going to be a clinical psychologist, you were going to help people. You were never, ever, going to get married. It was off the table. It was your final year at university and your dreams, like all of our dreams, were big and bright and calling us forth.

We met with some of your friends, artists, activist, photographers, you introduced me as a writer at Polet. I liked that, playing the role of the cool, erudite hipster swinging through the happening scenes of Novi Zagreb. Later we went to Korzo with everyone and talked and argued about the disappointments our generation suffered under Tito, the hope we all had for a new era faded when he crushed our Croatian Spring. The drab greyness of the political scene contrasted wildly with the vibrant cultural upsurge in Zagreb's art scene. I was happy then, so engaged and intellectually stimulated, sexually alive and intoxicated by you, you Elena. You brought the fire to the snow.

The room is colder again, and I feel stiff. I get up to throw another log onto the fire and pour another glass of red wine. God, I haven't listened to The Clash in years and wonder how I got to this intellectual wasteland. I want to blame you, Elena. I want to point out your part in this final act or how your character motivated our actions in the last few years. I want to point a finger at you, Elena. I want you to know that your freedom was my prison. And the so-called freedom you so craved was something you couldn't handle. In the end, you are a very ordinary woman, you want what most people want: undying love and security.

Remember how you tore into me in front of everyone at Blato, the café everyone ate dinner at? Do you remember? Everyone who was anyone was there that night: Mladen Stilinović, Tomislav Gotovac, Sanja Iveković. They're all famous artists now, big names in Europe. I said, and I remember this clearly because up until that point I've never seen you enraged; it was sexy and infuriating. It was our first lover's quarrel. And it was public and caused everyone to take a stand. I simply made a statement that caused you to slam your glass of Cézar on the table and your voice cut through the din in the room:

I said women cannot handle libertarianism. I said it was not in their biological make-up to handle libertarianism.

You said it was because men made the rules. You quoted Betty Friedan and Gloria Steinem and you started a riot in Blato.

And now Elena? Is your life not living proof of the statement I made that night at the wooden table in Blato?

And the night with Goran, you see, you wanted to prove to me that you were the libertarian, Elena. That night with Goran was initiated by you and your need for the world to see you as a free spirit. You never wanted to be the catholic girl conforming to Croatian values. You've seen what that does to women, your own mother getting beaten by her husband and life itself. That was not your deal. You were going to play your cards differently, you stated it publicly that night in Blato. It started with Goran, both of you wanted liberation and now, look at us now?

You accused me of being conformist when I wanted to settle in Zagreb, you laughed and laughed when I spoke about buying a house in Novi Zagreb. You accused me of being conformist, bourgeois even.

I know I should probably check if you arrived safely. I should call you but right now I'm angry: So angry about so many things, Elena.

I haven't thought of Zagreb or the country in years. I now visit it only occasionally, like one might visit an old lover, with fondness, but without the fire and passion that once burned and devoured.

I want to shut out the silence. I play Leonard Cohen's Chelsea Hotel. Self-indulgent? Wallowing? Maybe. I think of Goran. I think of that night and what followed. How you needed me after that. How I suppressed everything I needed and how Goran turned his back on all of us. And now he's back. He appeared there on the steps like an angel. I didn't tell you immediately. I couldn't, I knew my angel was your Lucifer, your dark side, your suspicions confirmed. And me? I still hoped, held out for my dream, my bourgeois, conformist dream, and now he's back.

It's strange recalling that night. I cannot say that it evokes or stirs up feelings. I know that it was a heady night, but that was more about the events before. It was a big night in Zagreb, you have to admit, we've never witnessed anything like it? And maybe that was part of it, who knows. It is difficult to describe that Zagreb to the new generation. Intellectualism mingled freely with art and followed us into bars and art galleries. Those were places people met up and talked about ideas. Am I accusing this generation of vacuousness? Probably. Sometimes I think the smartest thing about people now are their smartphones. It was different then, you said so many times. But then life gets in the way and who has time to discuss concepts and theories when we're dealing with feelings, broken hearts and staying alive?

You see, that's the problem: the shift to individualism and how we all matter. Maybe it started then. What was his name, the curator that changed everything, God, he really put the Student Centre Gallery on the map. Želimir Koščevic, that was his name. I mean he did what no-one else did in art galleries back then. And I was part of that. Polet paved the way with its editorial; it was Zagreb's NME magazine. My boss Pero Kvesić wrote the cult novel of the time: An Introduction to Pero K. I know you accused him of narcissism, Elena, but come on, he was an intellectual powerhouse. And he gave me my break as a writer. He sent me to interview Pankrti, the first punk band in Eastern Europe and that was a really big deal, you know that. And it was my article that inspired Želi to invite them to perform at the opening of the winter exhibition at the Student Centre Gallery.

There are nights in every life that stand out for some reason. Well, in most people's lives a night like the one we had would stand out. Your leather jacket and again the velvet hat, your long legs in the flared jeans. We were so much younger then. Electric, voltaic, galvanic, any of these words can describe the atmosphere at the gallery that night. Every corner, every space was filled with gyrating bodies, the walls full of contemporary art heralding a sea change in the culture. We were backstage because of my Polet pass. I held you close, and we danced and laughed with Mladen, Sanja and Goran and the other young people back stage. Goran's work was close to the entrance and you loved it immediately. Huge big red canvasses with intricate detail and textures. It was bold, provocation with an aesthetic beauty. You knew him from bumping into him at Blato and Korzo. He did stand out with his dark Slavic looks, his beard and piercing blue eyes.

We didn't want to leave after the show, we were so pumped up and energized after the last notes fell, the evening simply had to go on. We all went to KSET, all musicians always hung out there, the band was there as well. You and Goran started talking and Elena, I knew you fancied him, you loved his attention, his attentive manner. You flattered him, stroked his ego and spoke non-stop about his paintings. You said they spoke to you on an intellectual level. Something Goran always found irresistible.

Did I like him? Yes, Goran is charming, talented and has something mysterious about him. A strange dichotomy of libertarian and deep Catholicism, an incongruity that's both unsettling and hugely attractive. Did I object when you said he invited us back to his place? No, I thought it would be interesting to see more of his work through your lens, and anyway, I could do a piece on him for Polet. I have been to his place before, a few times. But that night was different.

The scene plays out in my mind like an old movie, like flashbacks through a camera lens. The Cézar bottle with the dark label and gold leaf pattern around the edges, the flickering fire light, the large white church candles are part of the scene. You and Goran next to each other on the wooden bench across the table, me on the other side. Your red lipstick, first on the glass then on Goran's lips. Your hand reaching out to me, his hand stroking my head. Later, on the bed, the white sheets, the arc of his back, the vertebrae, the muscular buttocks, him on top of you, you on top of me. Your pert breasts half obscured by your thick dark hair. In a way it was the perfect ending to a night. You were so light and smiling, laughing afterwards, I held you and we all fell asleep. The next morning Goran was already up, waiting for us with a freshly brewed coffee. The smell masked the crime of the previous night. You and I left after having the polite coffee. You were in a hurry for no reason.

You were silent on the tram over the Sava. You said you were just tired and had to go and shower and sleep.

You changed after that Elena. You called the next day and we had to meet. At Tingl Tangl we sat in the corner huddled and you wanted to talk about that night. I said it was your catholic guilt.

'No, it has nothing to do with that. I just…well, I just realized something Janick.' You started crying. I was confused. And then you said it: I love you. You said it for the first time.

I was taken by surprise and because I didn't respond immediately you got angry. It was always like that with you. Your anger when I don't react the way you expect. And when I said I couldn't go back to your place you accused me of enjoying the encounter with Goran more than having sex with you.

Can you see how you were not the libertarian you thought you were Elena? You were needy, you wanted my love, you wanted reassurance after Goran.

You started talking of leaving Zagreb, you said things were going to change politically. You wanted us to make a new life in Skopje after you graduated. I was happy at Polet, I was slowly making a name for myself. Pero liked my work. You grew restless. Skopje was our chance at meliora.

'I think you're a little bit in love with Goran.' You took my silence as confirmation. I felt every word from you was a trap, as if you made up your mind about me and my preferences. But it was your catholic guilt, it wasn't about me.

The last embers of the fire flickers. I pull the heavy throw from the back of the couch and cover myself. I feel warm, exhausted, disappointed and relieved. I wanted to call Goran. I wanted to tell him that it's all over between you and I, Elena, but I just don't know if it will make me feel better at this point. I know misery loves company, but I am speaking to you, in a way. I am trying to make sense of the mess we made in this house in Skopje. This is not a place where the word meliora can ever be used. It's impossible.

You might wonder why I never defended myself against Elena's accusations. Why I chose silence? You see, if I did tell you the truth about Goran and my history with him, you will accuse me of much worse. I never declared myself to be a libertarian. I was the conformist she accused me of being. I was a coward, there Elena, I admit it here in the presence of Leonard Cohen and the last flickers of the fire. I am a coward. But I never complained, and yes, I never explained.

What was the point? Goran left for the Vatican. Goran left. It was just you and me and a future I couldn't see, in Skopje.

WORLD OF TOMORROW

Two scoops of lemon ice cream for you. I looked back and watched you seated, waiting with your bag on your lap. I know you said water only, but I also know how much you love lemon ice cream. Strange, because I never fancied the fruit flavours.

I observed you for a minute from inside the shop. Sun rays cascaded down your black hair. Body physically present, but mind switched off. If I didn't know you well, I'd say you were meditating, but then you didn't know what meditation was. I watched you nervously rotating your marriage token on your ring finger, trying to organize your shattered thoughts, those same thoughts that aged you, in one place. You had said I wasn't an easy person to deal with, but tell me, mother, was understanding too much I asked from you?

'Your ice cream.'

'You didn't have to spend money.'

It was always money creating emotional indifference. Knowing your interest was limited to how much money we had spent, made, and how much we owed, I was surprised you didn't pull out one of the expense tracker notebooks you gave us for Christmas. 'Get rich quick' was your motto. If you only knew that this was going to be our last ice cream together, you wouldn't have told me not to spend money.

I sat and watched you stirring the ice cream in the bowl. I knew I had to start the conversation. 'I'm leaving.' A heavy silence fell on the cold marble table like a dead body. I could hear the wind blowing the mulch leaves behind you. I heard footsteps echoing, people laughing, some kissing, some hugging. I lost track of all of them. Were they nine people and one dog or one dog, nine people? I dragged my senses back to our table to face the darkness you brought, and there it was, tears sliding down your face as if your pain at last condensed into a deluge of rain. Your eyes were red, and so were mine. Just bloody say something.

'You hurt us.'

Let her speak; she needs this. It was your moment to scold me one last time. But no, you wanted to tell me about my father—the monster who called the cops on me for having my lover over. The man who was disgusted by my long bangs sat me on a chair and cut them. The man who beat me with a hose because I wasn't masculine like my brother.

'Your father was crying all night,' you said.

My father — pride possessed. When his father, my grandfather, died, he refused to get his body from my aunt's house. 'I didn't force him to spend the new year with her.,' he said about his long-hated sister. The night my grandfather was buried, a cry, similar to a cry of a child for a lost toy, kept me awake. Even then, at the age of twelve, I felt sorry for him.

'Is that all you have to say?' I asked.

You started inspecting your bag, and silence took over the table again. The night before, I dreamed of all of us seated together, laughing about the past, the mistakes we had made. In my sleep, all the pain we had caused to each other was gone. I was happy. WE were happy. But then you pulled a thin rectangular box from your hefty bag.

'What's this?' I asked.

'I worry you don't have pyjamas.'

The moment your words came out of your mouth, I realized my ice cream was completely melted, and you, you, had finally set me free. You came prepared. You wanted me gone. The next couple of minutes felt awkward. The silence joined us again, and wasn't planning to leave any time soon.

Seated, with a lump in my throat trying to fight back tears, I said, 'You haven't touched your ice cream.'

'Is it lemon?'

'Do you like it?'

'It's nice.'

In my dream last night, I said I was sorry. I was sorry for calling you stupid, but what was the point of saying sorry now? You cared more about what the neighbours might say than you cared for me. And even when I printed out research papers and begged you to read them, the neighbours' opinion was always more important. And did you even bother to read those papers to prove them wrong? To defend me, your son.

The chair became uncomfortable, and you tried to leave money for the ice cream. You never wanted people to pay for you. That was your way of saying you have to go. You stood up, bent over as if you were about to kiss me on my forehead, picked up your bag, and as you turned to walk away, you said, 'Call me from China.'

I watched you again in disbelief, and this time, the sun was gone. Your hair turned darker. You abandoned me. This time, your bag was on your shoulder, slowly dissipating in the crowd. It was just me and my dear friend, the silence.

JANIE RICHARDSON

I'm Janie and I'm 24. I studied health and social care at Bachelor level but couldn't stop writing random stories and fanfiction so picked Creative Writing back up the moment I could. I was born in Shropshire but I have an American twang to my accent. (My mum thinks it's because I watched a lot of American TV as a kid.) I love writing about magical worlds with fantastical creatures. I love superheroes, mermaids, space pirates and dragons. I'm 24 but I'm mentally about 12? I live in my own little worlds and spend any spare moment planning stories in my millions and millions of notebooks. I also draw a bit but I'm not great at that. I love cartoons and make great American pancakes that I've not perfected the art of flipping quite yet. For weekly updates on that, follow my Instagram- @Janiemrich. I tend to write Young Adult fantasy/Sci Fi novels and my favourite authors include Rick Riordan, April Daniels and Zordaida Córdova.

TAILED

This is an extract from a fantasy, young adult novel that I begun writing over summer. It follows a young girl named Lexi who lives in a beach town in the UK. She's selfish, spoiled and very much into her looks. She doesn't really know who she is or like her friends. She'd do anything for her little brother but that's it. One day, she's out at the beach and is caught by a witch who believes she needs to learn a lesson. She curses her and transforms her. The story follows her to a new world where she makes new friends and learns that life can be so much more than how other people see her and being friends with people who don't truly care for her.

Sleeping was hard. I felt stiffer and dryer than I'd ever felt. Every angle was oddly uncomfortable and breathing felt like I was forcing breaths out with a straw. It got harder and harder as the night wore on but I refused to open my eyes.

I mean, I obviously knew what was down there. I could feel the couch cushions scraping against the scales and the fins but having my eyes closed made me feel a little better, okay? I didn't even know how this happened or what was going to happen tomorrow. What would a scientist do if they saw me like this? What would my friends do? No, no they were never seeing this. I didn't want my parents or anyone seeing this. They'd only seen this because of that stupid tracker on my phone and the fact that I passed out. Why did I pass out? Urgh! Not remembering this was infuriating.

What had I done to deserve this crap? Had I done anything even remotely, just what even was this stupid thing? Okay, my eyes did open at that thought as all the rage in my mind floated to the surface.

I could barely see anything in the deep, dark light but I swear my skin was glowing. My skin, my eyes, my hair ... I don't know but looking at my hands and my stomach was causing strangled huffs to escape my lips. Why was I glowing? Was I a freakin night light now? I looked like a goddamn ghost! Didn't help that I was scarily pale. I was almost sheet white, even in the dull white light shining through me. I huffed again then shoved my lower half further into the couch, gulping as a strange sensation hit the back of my head.

I could feel it. It didn't feel right though? It felt like I had no bones below my waist somehow. The things on the end felt how it felt when you scraped the balls of your feet on something. It was slightly numb-er than the other things but I could still feel it, there was still a sense going through the back of my head. I currently had it covered with a little blanket but in all honesty, I don't think that was helping this drying feeling. It felt like my whole body was burning, it was yearning for something but I really didn't want to give it what it wanted. I didn't even know how I would. I couldn't even move.

It took a couple hours of me grunting and breathing painfully as my body continued to dry and solidify like I was in an oven for me to concede that the blanket was NOT helping. I gulped then gently and awkwardly, due to the claws, pushed the blanket onto the floor. My eyes closed instantly as a rush of relief hit me and the cold air of the living room flowed through my lower half. My heart started to calm and breathing got a little easier before I opened my eyes and both things stopped. Well, my heart started beating a mile a minute and breath got caught in my throat as I desperately tried to force out even a puff.

It gleamed at me in the dull white light protruding from every pore in my body. It actually gleamed brighter than any part of my body. The scales glimmered a light, sea blue like my eyes while the fins at the end glowed an insanely bright white. The scales covering my chest in a strange, little bra-like format also glimmered blue over me. I gulped down a hard breath and another and another and another as I just slowly and shakily trailed a finger along the edges of it.

A gasp escaped me as the dried-up circular things sent an odd signal through my brain and I watched on in slow motion shock as it jumped. It jumped a couple inches off the couch cushions and I shoved my hand into my chest, feeling my heart trying to pound through it.

Urgh, how was this happening? Why me? This was just ... whyyyy? I hated how real it felt. How real it looked. If it looked fake, at least I could pretend it was a costume or something? I don't know. What was ... what did I do to deserve this ridiculous thing? It wouldn't be so goddamn bad if my parents weren't my parents. At least, my friends would help ... if I ever even dared to show them which I was never going to. I would live in a box in a cave before I ever allowed them near this ridiculous thing.

Was this just me? Was I a fish freak ... forever? Almost drown in the ocean once and boom! Tail. How was that fair? People almost drown every day ... where the hell was their tail? I hmphed then glared down at the thing before closing my eyes again and turning into the couch cushions, deliberately ignoring the strain as the stupid thing tried to follow me. It just laid there, the cool air lapping it like the waves as I forcefully and angrily slept. My clawed fingers digging into the leather cushions as my eyes closed strongly.

Light quickly bled through my eyelids as a weirdly warm, wet thing hit my Left shoulder blade. My eyebrows lowered in confusion as I wiggled my back slightly, sensing five little ... were those ... my eyes snapped open as I turned around slowly. My heart stopped immediately as daylight gleamed through all the windows, hitting the scales and causing them to glow a bright, burning rainbow.

"Uh ... you just um ... you looked thirsty?" Danny's gentle, small voice suddenly muttered as I desperately tried to catch my breath. I stared at the tail and slowly leaned up; dragging it across with me, the strange sensation flooding the back of my brain as my heart only got faster. My back now leaned into the cushion as the kid just focused on my face. He held a large cup of water that was dripping slightly on the floor, every drop echoed through my mind and caused that weird, desperate yearning to get worse. The stupid blue thing was practically gagging for it as this point.

"Uh ... I ... uh ... thank you." I gasped slowly then took the glass from him. He smiled a little smile then gently sat on the couch beside me as I quickly chugged the water. My eyes closed tightly as a deep sigh of relief swam all over me. My limbs suddenly felt alive again as my heart began to flutter and before I knew it, the glass was empty.

Danny's light blue eyes then trailed my tail as I awkwardly placed the glass on the floor.

"Whoa." He gasped then poked it with his stubby finger. A pained, muffled feeling strangled my brain as the thing jumped up and I huffed, my hair jumping up with the breath. Danny's eyes went wide as he slowly and shakily got up off the couch. "It's ... uh ... it's ..."

"It's okay, Danny." I muttered gently with my hands out. "Calm down. It's still just ... um ..." My eyes glanced the scaly limb again as my heart jabbed through my ribs. "Me." I gasped.

"Lex?" The boy asked. I gulped and nodded to him. He just shook his head quickly, his eyes never leaving it as he sat back down beside me. "Sorry for um ... for poking it ... uh ... you." He stated, nervously wringing his fingers.

"It's uh ... it's okay." I muttered as the boy found my eyes again.

"What ... uh ... what happened?" He asked slowly.

"I ... uh ... I'm not uh ... I'm not sure." I stammered, my hand going to my chest as I felt my heart desperately trying to break through it. "I was just ... uh ... I was in the water yesterday and I don't uh ... I don't remember what ..."

"Alexandra Leigh Curtis! Put that blanket back on now or so help me! You're scaring your little brother!" Mum's shrill voice suddenly yelled from upstairs as I felt the blood leave my face and my eyes slowly lost Danny's as my back hunched.

"She's not ... uh ... she's not scaring me." Danny's voice muttered weakly. I smiled lightly then side-eyed him as he smiled back.

"While that is sweet of you, son." Mum's voice continued as she walked down the stairs. Her heels clicking the floor harshly as dread settled through the back of my mind. "Alexandra, cover yourself." She muttered then towered over me. Her deep green irises glaring through me as my heart leapt into my throat. "No one else is allowed to see this ... mutation, this freak thing. It's disgusting." My eyes fell to the floor where the blanket was as I gulped. It was disgusting, wasn't it? What was I thinking taking that blanket off? "And we are fixing it today." My eyes blinked back up to her.

"Uh, how?" I asked quickly with a disbelieving eyebrow.

"I don't care how ... I'm not having a fish for a daughter." She stated pompously as my eyes rolled.

"I feel fine, thanks for asking ... by the way." I muttered as mum stalked into the kitchen. "Nah, the scales and the fins don't feel at all weird and I'm not starving or thirsty or freaked out in anyway ..." I continued to mutter as Danny trailed my face. He lightly got up from the couch and gently handed me the blanket.

"It's not disgusting." He whispered then went after my mother. I blinked in surprise as my fingers gripped the little blanket. My eyes then found the tail again as the daylight gleamed off it. Maybe, it was kind of pretty? I quickly shook my head then lowered my eyebrows in annoyance as I chucked the blanket over it. The warmth quickly trailed me and made me feel instantly uncomfortable as a growl escaped my lips.

"God, I hate this thing." I muttered as my eyebrows lowered. How on earth was mum going to fix it? Didn't matter, she was going to. ANY thing was better than this. I couldn't even freakin' walk! And it just ... felt so wrong and gross, where did my leg bones go? Where did any of it go? It just ... seriously, what did I do to deserve this crap?

Danny came back a moment later with a bowl of coco pops and another glass of water. He placed them gently on the coffee table before me before picking up the glass and passing it to me. A warm feeling struck my heart as I gently took it off him. "Thank you." I whispered. He grinned at me.

"The cereal is for you too but can you ... uh ..." He began then awkwardly looked to the bowl then to me. My eyebrows lowered as I caught his drift. Could I actually move to get the bowl? Yeah, probably not.

"I mean, probably not?" I gulped. Danny smiled lightly.

"Just let me know when you want it." He stated then sat down beside me as I started chugging another glass of water. My eyes closed tighter as I felt it ripple through me and a warm, wonderful feeling flooded my heart as the cool liquid slapped the back of my throat. Danny suddenly gasped. "Whoa." I opened my eyes quickly, glass still in hand. His blue eyes found mine. "You're uh ... you're glowing." I gulped then looked down at my white, shining arms as a shiver rang over me and my eyes glared down at the stupid fins. I mean, of course I was. Just, urgh.

"Right." My voice growled. "Can I have the cereal please?" Danny smiled lightly then handed me the bowl as I awkwardly placed the glass back on the floor. My clawed fingers surrounded the cool ceramic as Danny's blue eyes shot open wide. He shook it off when I noticed him staring but I couldn't blame him. I mean, I've had long nails before but they were pink, blunt, fake and covered in little silver rhinestones. They weren't threatening in the slightest. These things? Stretched about three or four inches out of my fingers; were a stark, bluish-black; pointed like daggers and gleamed dangerously in the daylight. They tapped the sides of the bowl as I gripped the cool material and a line of white-hot pain stabbed through the back of my brain as I felt one bend back. I gulped it down then very gingerly grabbed the spoon; my nails awkwardly surrounding the silverware. I could feel it slipping through my fingertips so I decided to basically inhale my coco pops. Spoonful after spoonful after spoonful. I choked maybe five times? But the bowl was cleaned and my spoon didn't fall out my claws so, I think I won. I mean, if you took out the whole 'I was currently a mutant freak with a fish tail' thing. Danny gently took the bowl off me as I heavily swallowed my last mouthful. "Thanks bro." I muttered. He smiled lightly to me.

"Daniel! Why aren't you ready for school?!" Dad's deep voice suddenly boomed and my eyes shot wide open as the thick, dark-haired man with the perfectly combed moustache appeared down the stairs. His blue eyes glared angrily at my little brother and my heart panged as Danny wilted. A deep sigh escaped my throat. I mean, it's not like they could be more disgusted by me, right?

"It was my fault, dad." I stated simply. "I asked Danny to get me breakfast." Danny turned his panicked eyes on me as his mouth flapped open and closed like a fish. I just smiled at him then turned to the man on the stairs. He wore his black suit as usual with the slim black tie and his ridiculously shiny shoes. His short black hair was combed back with an insane amount of gel and I couldn't help the exasperated look that deflated through my eyes.

"Daniel, go get dressed." My dad snapped quickly to my brother. Danny jolted then turned to me. I just nodded, hoping that he caught my drift of 'I'll be fine, don't worry' and the boy smiled then sped back upstairs before the suited man sped down and stood before me. "So, Alexandra. Care to explain your current predicament?" He asked with a ... disappointed, frustrated tone? I couldn't tell but it wasn't friendly or caring. I felt like I was being berated by my school principal.

I stared down at the blue scales surrounding my chest and the little shells currently lining the blonde braids in my hair before a deep sigh echoed through me. "If I could explain it, I would." I muttered impatiently while glaring up at the man.

"Steven, is that you hon?" My mum's voice asked from the kitchen.

"Yes, Frankie." His serious voice muttered as his eyes still glared through me. His teeth biting in disgust.

"Can I borrow you for a moment?!" My mum yelled and a relieved sigh flew over me as the man stomped off into the kitchen.

The relief did not last long however as mum stepped back into the room, her giant heels clanking on the wooden floor as her eyes found me. "Okay, Alexandra. We're getting you in the car and we're going to the hospital." My eyes widened as I stared down at the tail then back up into my mum's intensely glaring eyes.

"The hospital? This isn't some sort of twenty-four fish tail flu, mum! It's not like anti-biotics are gonna do anything." My voice growled. My mum's glare deepened as her short, blonde page boy hair swirled around her face.

"Then what do you suggest?" She spat at me. I gulped then stared down at my hands and my chest then my hair before looking back up at her. "Just what I thought. Honey!"

My dad wondered back through with a long dress shirt in his hands and a bobble in his fingers. "Put these on." He commanded then handed them to me. I just looked at the objects then looked at my claws then back up to my parents.

"Yeah, I can't do that." I sighed. The adults just blinked dumbly at me until I pointed to my claws.

"For goodness' sakc." My mum grumbled then chucked the shirt over my shoulders before aggressively shoving my arms through the arm holes. I grunted as I felt my shoulder pop and my muscles twang. Both arms went through and she started doing up the buttons as my dad quickly chucked my long, wavy hair in a bobble, painfully tugging at every strand as I flinched. "There." My mum stated then leaned back while looking over me.

A wave of hot discomfort washed over my chest as my body protested the shirt ... and the blanket. Everything just felt too warm. My clawed fingers awkwardly went to my lips as I felt them start to dry out. A gulp rang over me as my parents grinned down at me. "Uh ... I don't think this is gonna work."

"Nonsense, just keep the blanket on. We'll get you a wheelchair once we get to the hospital." My dad stated as I stared at him.

"A wheelchair?" I asked. He nodded dumbly to me.

"Got a better suggestion for the girl with the tail? Can you walk on the glowing fins?" He spat the words 'tail' and 'fins' at me and I felt my heart fall back through my chest. This wasn't my fault. I don't know what happened but it's not like I wished for this. I stared up at my dad. His serious frown and glaring eyes were unwavering and it took me a moment to realise that he was actually waiting for an answer. I shrank into myself then stared at the floor.

"No." I muttered.

"Good." My mum stated happily. "Now, Steven ... grab her and we'll go." Grab her? What was I ... a suitcase? My dad hesitated for a moment while looking over me. His eyes quickly went to my tail and my claws as he nervously bent down before me.

A moment passed before he very awkwardly chucked my body over his shoulder. My head hit his chest while my tail flopped uselessly on his back. The look of disgust on his face was priceless but ... it hurt. It felt like a knife through the heart as my mum chucked the blanket over my lower half once more. "Okay." My father muttered seriously as the three of us wondered out the front door, my eyes wondering to the couch and to the stairs as I felt my heart collapse. Would this be the last time I saw this place?

JOANNA MANSFIELD

Joanna Mansfield lives in West Yorkshire. Though writing is her passion, she seems to spend more time avoiding it than doing it. She has been trying to write this biography for two weeks and has failed miserably.

GASLIGHTING

The sky is opaque and claustrophobic. Flakes have been falling for most of the night, gradually transforming the street from technicolour to monochrome. Some might call it pretty, but today I am unable to see past my disappointment. The cancellation of my trip is a major blow and more than just a postponed holiday. I need this break.

I can't face unpacking my little suitcase. In fact, I can't face another moment in this flat; I have to get away, even if only for a few hours.

As I struggle into my boots, he comes up behind me. I try not to flinch. I need to get out. Now.

'Just popping into town.' I pick up my keys, fling my bag over my shoulder and head for the door.

'How long will you be?'

'Not sure.' I'm deliberately vague as I don't want to give him any excuse to complain if I'm too long. 'I've got a few things to do.' I slip through the door and close it behind me before he has chance to reply. I don't stop walking until I reach the end of the street, my footsteps crunching perfect shoe prints into the virgin snow. Then I breathe.

I feel I am holding back a tsunami. An avalanche of clutter, threatening to bury me and everything I am. I needed this weekend away but it would have been a mixed blessing. I would have relaxed for a few days but returned to find the tide a few more feet up the metaphorical beach.

I wander round town, not wanting to be there but finding the idea of going home an unwelcome alternative. The Christmas decorations are still up in the shopping centre. Gaudy foil Santas grin down at the crowds of bargain hunters and tacky red and gold chains are strung across the wide walkways. This depresses me even more.

I return home to Gary drinking a cup of tea, reading the paper. Royksopp is playing full blast on the stereo. Without looking in the kitchen, I know that the pile of washing up will still be waiting for me.

'Oh, don't do that now, sweetie,' Gary says, having to raise his voice over the music. He knows where I am going without me having to say and is trying to lead me to the sofa. 'Sit down and have a cup of tea.'

I shrug off his arm. 'I'd rather get it done now, then I can relax.'

'Come and relax now.' He sits on the sofa and pats the space next to him. I ignore him and head for the kitchen, rolling the rubber gloves over my sleeves.

My little kitchen radio is no match for the swanky stereo in the next room, but nevertheless I turn it up as far as it will go, and the two fight for superiority. It's a petty move that punishes both of us, as the resulting noise is pleasant for no one. I find it strangely comforting, though. I spend the next half hour swishing warm soapy water, the smell of bitter coffee mingling with Fairy Liquid, singing along to the 'Sounds of the Eighties' at the top of my voice. The cat winds in and out of my legs, wanting dinner.

If Gary is annoyed, he doesn't show it. He comes in and makes me a cup of tea, even though I have given no indication I want one.

'Thanks.' I wipe down the surfaces with a cloth, or the part of the surfaces that remain exposed beneath the piles of newspapers, junk mail and unpaid bills.

'Come and sit down.'

'I'll be there in a minute. I just need to do this.'

He opens his mouth then shuts it again. After a pause he says, 'Don't throw away anything, will you?'

'I won't throw away anything important.'

If he notices my equivocation, he doesn't say anything. He goes back to his seat on the sofa. I tidy the clutter into various piles and sneak a couple of old newspapers into the recycling box. Next, I unpack a Tesco carrier bag full of tins and cupboard items that has been sitting on the worktop for days. Then I turn my attention to the hall. There is a new pile of secondhand books on the floor, either from the library's 'sale' shelf or the bookshop in Grove Road. Gary can't resist a cheap book, even if it is about something as uninteresting as cod fishing in the Atlantic. A red and black toolbox is overflowing onto the floor and various random objects lie strewn around: a bottle of mouthwash, two packs of Andrex, a Big Issue magazine, some cat toys, a phone charger.

I tidy up as best I can, but the problem is there is nowhere to put anything. Books are already double-stacked in the bookcases with piles on the floor in front. And Gary's obsession with buying tools simply leads to more homeless junk, rather than an increase in DIY projects.

I take the mouthwash and toilet rolls to the bathroom – at least those I can put away. Closing the bathroom door and sitting on the toilet lid, I revel in the silence and relative tidiness of the room. Here is the one place I can be alone.

It is August and I haven't been feeling myself for a couple of weeks. As I sit on the bath edge, I know before I look at the piece of plastic in my hand there will be two little pink lines in the results window. What other explanation could there be for puking my guts up all day and the death-like exhaustion? Ok, maybe quite a few, but I know my own body and I know that this is no ordinary 'illness'.

I don't know how to feel. I have wanted a baby for so long, but for some reason thought it would never happen. Now it just seems surreal. Gary and I are hardly ideal parents, and this flat is far from the best place to raise a child. And… As conflicting thoughts converge in my mind, I realise that there is one underlying emotion. Joy. It takes me by surprise.

Gary is happy too. We talk. He agrees that the flat needs to be sorted and that by the time the baby is born we will have a suitable home for her (I know I am having a girl. I can feel it). Of course, I believe him, and of course he has no intention of living up to his promises: we have been here so many times.

I am quite poorly during the pregnancy which means I am not able to keep up with the housework. Naturally, no one else does it. The hormones play havoc with my body and my brain. It is 1:00 am and ping! I am wide awake. This is one of the most annoying side effects of pregnancy: I fully expect sleep deprivation once the baby is born, but now it is just infuriating. I can hear the murmur of the TV in the next room, meaning Gary is still up. I can't stop thinking about the shambles the flat is in and know there is no way I will get back to sleep with it in this state.

I don't even make it to the kitchen before Gary is out of his chair and attempting to frogmarch me back to bed.

'What on earth are you doing? Do you know what time it is?'

I shrug myself free from his grasp. 'I can't sleep. I'm going to tidy up.'

'At this time of night? You're being ridiculous.' Again, he tries to lead me by the shoulders back to bed.

I want to tell him that what's ridiculous is the fact that he is just sitting there watching TV when there is so much that needs doing. The fact he knows I am stressing yet does nothing to tackle the root of what is stressing me. But he knows all this because we have had that conversation so many times, and despite being unable to sleep I am exhausted. I allow him to lead me back to bed, where he tucks me in and goes back to his TV.

I lie in silent rage until I have to get up again to go to the toilet. My sense of smell has become super sensitive and everything makes me puke. The chemical scent of the liquid soap in the bathroom is the worst; just one whiff and my stomach empties itself, no matter what time of day (or night). Gary is not open to changing the brand, even temporarily. I hurl into the toilet as tears run down my face. It is an involuntary reaction: I puke, I cry. But today the tears are more than just a physical response. Anger and frustration are erupting from deep inside me. I flush and feel little a better.

The flat continues to get messier and the baby's room still isn't ready. A month before my due date I have finished work and am officially on maternity leave. I am knackered and can barely move due to my stupid size.

Gary is still working every day, so on a Wednesday (bin day) I wait until he has left then scoot round that flat filling as many bin bags as I can with his junk. There is usually about twenty minutes between him leaving and the bin men arriving, and I am virtually unhinged as I race around the flat throwing whatever I can into a black sack, then heaving it into the wheelie bin. I repeat, until the bin is crammed, lifting far more than I should for someone in my condition. Do I worry that my actions will harm the baby? Of course, but I am like something possessed. I am compelled to make a decent home for my baby, even if doing so puts that baby at risk.

Gary never notices anything missing, which is a testament to how much useless crap he has. Four bin bags a week is but a drop in the ocean and I am still drowning.

The baby is here. The flat is a mess, but at least she has all the latest baby gadgetry.

I watch her sleep. Rosebud lips pressed gently together and arms flung above her head in a position of surrender. She couldn't be more adorable if a photographer had positioned her like this, in order to create a portrait entitled 'innocence'. She will still favour this sleeping position as she enters teenage years.

She takes my breath away, yet my love is edged with guilt. I have created a new life, brought this perfect child into a family that is damaged. The cracks in our relationship have become crevasses, and I cannot get a grip on my emotions. I want the world to be perfect for my daughter, yet I'm adrift.

'Do you want a cup of tea?' Gary has appeared at the door.

'No, I don't want a fucking cup of tea. I want a clean and tidy flat. I want an environment fit for a baby.'

Gary's 'stuff' has been expanding. His wardrobe is stuffed with newspapers, so his entire collection of clothing now lives in a heap on the bedroom chair. I have no idea what is clean and what is dirty. His bedside table cannot even be seen under a mountain of papers, gadgets and general rubbish that spills onto the floor and halfway to the door.

'Shhhh…' he admonishes. 'You'll wake her.'

I leave the room as I have no volume control at the moment. I have little control of any kind.

In the lounge I sink into the armchair and put my head in my hands.

'Oh, what's the matter now?' He has followed me.

'You know what the matter is.'

'For fuck's sake. Not this again.'

'Yes. This again. And it will continue to be "this again" until it is resolved.'

'You act as if I'm out with another woman every night.'

'To me that would be preferable. At least it wouldn't affect my home and my baby's environment.'

'Oh, now you're being ridiculous. This environment is normal! Stop being such a damn clean freak.'

'How can I be a clean freak when you won't even let me clean?' I try a different tack. 'Can we at least go for counselling? Try and sort out our relationship?'

'There's nothing wrong with our relationship. You're the one with psychological problems. You really need to sort yourself out. Honestly, love, this isn't healthy.'

I am infuriated that he can remain so calm when I am struggling to speak. I stand up and grab my coat off the hook.

'Now where are you going?'

'For a walk.' I slam the front doo, then regret it, hoping I haven't woken the baby.

It is almost Christmas, and I am sitting on a bench watching the sea. I spend most of my days walking up and down the seafront with the pram or trying to spin out a cuppa for a couple of hours in Debenham's café. Anything to avoid the flat. Some days I manage to convince myself that Gary is right – I am the one with the problem. We could have a normal, happy relationship if I wasn't the one jeopardising it.

I watch TV programmes about extreme hoarders and realise he isn't that bad after all. At least we don't have to mountaineer over a pile of junk to get through the front door or scrape away layers of mould in order to have a bath. And like he says, he has always been faithful. And he loves me. He is always telling me that.

I cannot walk through the shopping centre at the moment. Everything is too bright, too loud and too Christmassy. It sends me into a panic. I try not to think about the oodles of presents we will receive in just a few days' time. Where on earth are we going to put them all?

It is too cold to sit for long so I get up and continue walking. The sea is a bitter grey and the sky is threatening rain. There is no one else around. I know it will be a different story in the town centre, where most of the town's population are finishing off their Christmas shopping.

The baby – Amelia – is wrapped up in a white Winnie the Pooh snow suit and looks very cute. A twinge of sadness eats at my stomach. It soon turns into guilt. I should be enjoying this time and savouring every second, not wallowing in self pity. And what must my outbursts be doing to the baby? She is old enough now to understand that Mummy is being cross and shouty. What on earth must she think of me?

I turn the pram homeward and resolve to stop being such a mardy cow.

The car is rammed to the roof, but there are still fragments of my life that will not fit. They have to stay behind but in time will not be missed. The baby, snuggled in her car seat in the back, seems content enough within her cocoon of bric a brac.

There is an unexpected delay when Gary takes Amelia from me and shuts himself in the bedroom with her. After staring at the door for a few seconds I follow them in. He is hunched on the bed, arms wrapped tightly around my daughter. I pick my way through the discarded clothes on the floor and reach for her, but his grip tightens. He gives a gulp and a sob, and I realise he is crying. This is new, and I don't know how to deal with it.

'Please give her to me.' I hear the tremor in my voice.

He clings to her tightly, like a lost child hugging a teddy bear, and sobs. It is the most emotion I have seen him express in the whole thirteen years we have been together. I would have given anything at one time to see the slightest sign that he cared, but now it is too little far too late. Eventually, I manage to prise Amelia from his grasp. He continues to sit there, head down, shoulders shuddering. I leave him to wallow alone.

I buckle the baby into her car seat and take my place in the front beside my father. My cheeks are wet from the tears I had been unable to stem, but I hastily wipe them as I fasten my seatbelt. Crying – or, indeed, any kind of emotional display – is something my father cannot abide. I gaze out of the window at the closed front door as we drive away, pretending I am fine, wondering when – if ever – I will return. Things have been said. Horrible things that cannot not be unsaid. But in time could there be forgiveness, or, failing that, civility?

I feel the urge to see the sea one last time, but not wanting to risk a fresh flood of tears I say nothing as we drive out of town and towards the motorway. My father glances at me.

'Are you OK?'

I nod but say nothing, not trusting my voice to remain even.

Service stations become markers between nappy changes and feeds: South Mimms, Peterborough, Leicester Forest. We don't talk about what has happened. As the day wears on, I try to chat normally as if my life hasn't just fallen apart. I try not to think of the ever-increasing distance between myself and almost everything that means anything to me. Will our friends feel they have to take sides? Will I be left with anyone?

The sun hangs low in the sky for most of the journey but disappears from view late afternoon. The temperature in the car seems to drop. I am impatient to be somewhere, anywhere.

We pull up at our destination as darkness gains a foothold on the day: a house in a leafy suburb far away from the sea. I lift out the baby and walk up to the front door. A warm glow seeps out from the closed curtains and a tabby cat sits on the doorstep, licking its front paw. For the first time I feel reconciled to my situation. Homeless, but not without a home.

THE BIG ISSUE SELLER: A MODERN FAIRYTALE

Snow was falling but it was not magical. The unblemished flakes dissolved into grime-mingled slush, churned by the footfall of countless shoppers whose urgency was compounded by the close proximity of Christmas Day. Figures wrapped in warm layers hurried from store to store, heads down against the flurry of snowflakes, paying little attention to the magazine seller standing in the middle of the precinct.

The young woman could no longer feel her hands, one of which was frozen into a claw around her stack of magazines. 'Big Issue,' she called. 'Happy Christmas.' But her cries were ignored. She had no gloves and her feet were in flimsy shoes, unsuitable for such bitter weather. The thin coat she wore did little to keep out the scathing wind.

Darkness had begun to seep into the afternoon, dirtying the air. The woman coughed. A dry, hacking cough that she had had for weeks and really needed medical attention, but when did she have time to see a doctor? A moment away from the High Street was potentially a missed sale, even though most of the day could pass without a single interaction between herself and her would-be benefactors. No, she could not risk it. She was already berating herself for spending the proceeds of this morning's one, precious sale on a cup of coffee, even though it was the only thing she had consumed all day. Had she known that it would be all she would sell, she wouldn't have been so frivolous. If she made no more money, how would they eat tonight? How would she feed the baby? She couldn't think like that. She had to sell more.

'Big Issue!' she shouted. 'Big Issue! Merry Christmas to you and your family!'

She did her best to hide her thick accent, but her voice was an instant indicator of her heritage. Is this how she had imagined her new life in the UK would be before she set off on this punishing journey? There was no work in Romania, but at least there was family. She thought of her mother, hovering over the stove for hours, the savoury smell of her famous rasol filling the kitchen. What she would give for a bowl of her mother's hot stew now. And her father. Dear Papa! She remembered him teaching her to make daisy chains when she was little and helping her with her schoolwork. He sat with her for hours at the kitchen table, patiently explaining the parts she didn't understand. She had always been a Papa's girl.

But then her father lost his job and there wasn't enough food to go round. She had wanted to study to be a teacher, but it wasn't fair that she should be a burden on the family. The little ones were still at school; they couldn't go out to work, but she could.

It was Erik, her cousin, who had arranged the job in England. How full of hope she had been when she came over to Leeds by coach, eager to make her family proud. How quickly that hope had dissipated when she found there was no sign of Erik and no job. She ended up eating from bins and sleeping on pavements, where she quickly blended in with the other homeless of the city. Ashamed of her situation, she could not tell her parents what had happened. She simply did not contact them.

At least now she had the Big Issue job and somewhere to live, but it was far from the life she had envisaged. But she also had Ivan and the baby, and thinking of them made her feel warm inside, despite the cold despair eating at her heart. Picturing them in the little room they shared made her smile. It wasn't much, but it was clean and dry. Sparsely furnished, with bed, table, two dining chairs and a battered chest of drawers, there was also a fridge and a tiny stove on which they could heat beans or soup. When they couldn't afford to put money in the meter, they ate it cold and huddled together on the bed for warmth. During a particularly cold spell last winter, she had learned to knit and made a huge blanket with colourful wool she found in a charity shop. All three of them huddled together under it on cold evenings.

She wanted to go home, but she could not go back to her husband with nothing. Ivan would say it was okay, that she had done her best, but it was not okay. She was the... what did the English call it? The breadwinner. Though today, ironically, she had not enough for even the smallest loaf.

Tonight, they may not be able to heat their room, but she would make sure they had something to eat. If she could sell just two more copies of the magazine, she could buy some tinned soup then go home.

With new resolve she shouted, 'Big Issue! Please buy magazine!'

Would it be any different if she had been born and bred in the UK? Somehow, she couldn't see those hurrying past suddenly forming a queue to give her their hard-earned cash, even if she spoke the Queen's English. She may as well have been invisible.

A lady with a small child glanced her way, then glanced away.

'Big Issue?' She held out one of the magazines to the woman's retreating back. 'Please buy. I have family. I have baby at home.'

The lady and child hurried on. It was hopeless. She coughed again, her slender body bent and spent with exhaustion. A layer of snow had settled on her head and arms, but she couldn't shelter in the shop doorways or under awnings – the owners didn't like it and moved her on.

Leaning against a lamppost, she sank to the floor, just needing to sit a while. She'd be okay in a minute but she just needed a moment. People passed by but didn't notice or didn't care, as the young woman lay her head on the ground, dreaming of summer meadows and pine trees and freshly-baked walnut cookies. Eyes closed, there she stayed on the frozen ground as the new flakes covered her in a blue-white shroud.

And that was where her husband found her three hours later, papers strewn all around her. He had become concerned when she didn't arrive home and gone out to look for her, carrying the baby in a papoose. He wept when he saw her and felt for a pulse. It was weak, but it was there. Filled with hope, he shook her and shouted, but try as he might he could not get her to open her eyes. Hope departed. He sank to the floor and wrapped his body around hers, the baby in between them. No one disturbed them all night until an ambulance was finally called by a man walking his dog in the early morning.

The woman was already stiff and cold, her spirit having drifted away as she lay in the arms of those she loved. Her husband was still alive but died a few hours later, the call of his wife's spirit too strong to resist. The baby was suffering from mild hypothermia but expected to survive, having been kept safe in the hollow of warmth between her parents.

JESSICA KELLY

Jessica Kelly is an aspiring writer who started writing fantasy fiction at the age of 13. She enjoys reading sci-fi/fantasy and she has a notebook addiction that her mother cites is "a problem". The piece she has written in this anthology is about her grandfather, a man she credits as her role model and the father-figure in her life. She wrote this piece about the heartbreaking moment her grandfather was diagnosed with cancer to capture the despair such a diagnosis causes, as well as the love she has for her grandfather. She has two horses, two dogs, and three cats that like to lay across her keyboard and notebooks when she's writing.

Jess applied for the MA in Creative Writing not realising it was a Master's degree. Having not completed any previous degrees, she decided to go for it anyway in the hopes that it would help her produce her original story idea further, which she one day hopes to see published. In her spare time, she also enjoys gaming, drawing, and tends to redecorate her house at least once a month.

A Cancerous Memory

Her voice faded into the distance. The rest of what she said didn't register. All I could focus on was that one word.

Cancer.

The room was on stilts. Or maybe I was. Everything was spinning, and my mind had gone into overdrive. Air was scarce, vision blurring, heart pounding like a jackhammer. *Cancer.*

'Miss Kelly?'

I could hear the doctor, but my focus was on my grandfather. His face was ashen, his gaze void of any thought or emotion, and mouth set ajar, as if he'd been about to speak and only silence had come out. Normally, his thick Irish accent would fill the room, unstoppable and full of humour. There'd be a witty quip, usually followed by an unusual fact he'd recall from out of nowhere. He once informed me, 'A person can't sneeze in their sleep.' I'd laughed, then fact-checked him online to find him correct, as usual. For a man of eighty-seven, his mind was incredible.

Suddenly, he appeared his age, all of his brilliance sucked dry once those words left the doctor's mouth. He'd aged before my eyes, the air around him stale.

Realisation dawned. Weakness was not an option; I needed to be strong. It was the reason my grandfather wanted me here; to take in all the information and understand what was happening to him. The sudden weight loss; the prolonged aches and pains; random bouts of sickness… so many symptoms over the last six months. Symptoms the professionals had struggled to diagnose. We'd seen it all before in my grandmother, and yet no one listened when I dared utter *cancer*. As if it couldn't possibly be happening to my grandfather as well.

One in two people. Five people in the family so far. In all our experience dealing with this disease, all the countless hospital visits, even a funeral…. This one hurt the most. It was hard to put to words the feeling that washed over me each time. The all-too-familiar sensation of dread, gathering like a thunderous cloud at the end of a hot summer's day.

The aseptic smell of the hospital knocked me back into the present. My vision blurred from the glaring white walls of the room; the ticking of the clock too loud to my ears; the fruity smell of the doctor's perfume overpowering, making it hard to breathe. Overhead, the light flickered for the briefest moment. My chest tightened as I forced my stinging eyes upon the doctor.

'Where do we go from here?' I forced the words from my dry lips.

Beside me, my grandfather briefly stirred, the sound of my voice bringing him back from the brink of wherever he had been. My fingers twitched from the unyielding urge to reach out, to reassure him, but I couldn't move. I wanted to take this pain away from him; I just didn't know how.

The doctor nodded gratefully, her expression understanding and unbearably sympathetic. 'It's a discussion the specialist team will have. They'll need to see if the cancer has spread, which will require a CT scan.'

The onset of stress and fear was like a haze threatening to overcome me the longer we sat in this room. Pins and needles prickled across my skin, spreading like wildfire, leaving heat in its wake. My fingers dug into the arms of the seat, nails bending from the pressure. I'd leaned forward at some point, hovering over the edge of the chair, ready to spring into action.

The need to escape that enveloped me grew stronger.

'When will we hear from them?' *Can this be cured? How long do we have? Please tell me if my granddad will be okay?*

So many questions burning.

'They will discuss it in the Friday meeting,' she explained. 'They'll call you Monday.'

The injustice of it all.

The surge of adrenaline coursing through me sent my heart into overdrive again. I saw red. Common sense told me this flood of rage wasn't aimed at this doctor or any person in particular, but I could feel the outburst building. The need to vent, to cry and lash out was frightening; never before had emotion ruled me in this way. A vision sprang to mind; of letting loose with screams and abuse, flinging chairs; blaming anyone in the way. It would be the quickest way to release this pressure on my chest. Would that make this cancer disappear? I couldn't lose my granddad. He'd helped raise me. He was a father to me. He'd filled a void left by an unworthy man. A guiding light throughout my childhood.

With feet pressed hard to the floor in concentration, I fought to steady myself. This hospital visit was drastically different to the last one. He'd had low potassium the last time we were here. Set up on a drip, he was the life of the ward, making everyone around him laugh when the nurse asked how he liked his cup of tea.

'Just like how my mother used to make,' he'd said. 'And that's why I left home.'

My stomach hurt from the laughter. The nurse called him cheeky. My grandfather was pale, weak, and struggling to sit, but his own laughter had been louder than ever.

The thought brought tears to my eyes. I blinked furiously to remove them, trying to ignore the ache. *Calm down. Don't let him see you like this.*

Then, memories of my childhood blinded me in rapid succession. Being pushed on a swing, my grandfather laughing and singing Irish tunes I barely understood. He'd push me as high as he could, while I kicked my legs in glee, trying to fly. Our races to the slide, where he'd patiently wait at the bottom, while I fought to climb to the top. My first taste of black pudding, served specially by him; I'd greedily ate it, relishing the strange taste, while he slowly explained what, exactly, it was. His guffaw rang loud, hazel eyes twinkling with keen mischief as I'd stopped mid-bite to gape at him. When I threatened to vomit, he clipped my ear. 'You're grand, wolf it down you!' It soon became our shared favourite; he'd order it specially, all the way from Ireland, and cook it for me every weekend. Growing up, I struggled to understand him a lot of the time. He'd speak fast, sometimes mutter insults in Gaelic, and often mumbled if he wanted to fade into the background in a crowded room. The one thing you could never steal from him was his pride; if he overheard someone discussing something of importance, he'd spring back into view and fall into a polite debate. He enjoyed standing up for what was right, no matter who it was against. We used to spend hours at the pub, chattering and drinking away, him with a pint and me with a coke, until his doctor advised he stop with the alcohol; a curse to any Irishman's ears. He had the willpower to do it, though. To do anything he wanted. He cut out sugar, started eating healthily, and exercised more... *For what? To get cancer at the very end?*

Adored by many for his humour, knowledge and caring nature, and moreover renowned for his strong will and quick decision-making, my grandfather was a one-in-a-million. Family meant everything to him. *He* meant everything to me.

Which was what made this so much harder. Sitting beside him, accepting that he, my favourite person in this whole damn world, had cancer.

What a cruel world. It fractured my belief in a God.

I finally looked at him. He turned to me. We stared for a moment, lost in the memories we shared. I couldn't begin to imagine how we were going to tell my grandmother.

That's when I saw it. That look of knowing on his face; the thought that was possessing him. He was scared, yes, but I suddenly knew what terrified him the most.

Leaving us behind.

I could imagine the images of my grandmother flashing through his mind. Imagining her struggling to live without him, wheelchair-bound from losing one leg to cancer. He was protective of her. He did everything he could for her. He never wanted to leave her behind.

The glistening in his eyes made my chest tighten. I held back more tears of my own and smiled sadly. This news wasn't what we wanted, but we wouldn't let it end here.

Inwardly, I made a promise.

I reached out and grabbed his hand, and watched in bitter silence as his tears started to fall.

PT REYNOLDS

PT Reynolds is the author of two books and is working on historical fiction, short story, and creative non-fiction projects.

Reynolds recently completed a Masters in Creative Writing, with a First in multiple assignments. That was 25 years after a Bachelors Degree in Politics and failed bids to be elected as Student Union President and get a commission in the Army. His prior careers were in marketing, the church, and as a homemaker. That, living in the Caribbean, and being half-Dutch and half-English, gives him a vast and diverse reservoir of characters and situations to draw on.

He is now a full-time writer, which is the job he wanted since the age of five.

Born to a Dutch mother and English father. He lives with his wife, a dog, two cats, and an indeterminate quantity of fish. He aspires to be as gifted or focused as either his marvellous wife or one of their two superb children.

THE PROBLEM WITH TEENAGE BOY LIONS

Ezekiel stopped our open-sided, open-top jeep about ten yards from what looked like a disturbance in the long grass. When he turned off the engine we could hear the rustling, in bursts, becoming louder.

"It's a mother and her son", he said.

"He's getting frisky with her and she's not having it."

We took a few seconds to process that, and his words were perfectly clear, but I had to ask,

"Say that again?"

"The young male lion wants to…have his mother. She has to discipline him."

I would think so. Mum was quite capable of taking care of herself it seemed, and give her teenage-equivalent son a good thrash and scratch to send him packing.

"Is that…normal?"

"Yes", Ezekiel replied cheerily. "It will get worse, and eventually his father will attack him so he has to leave the family, leave the pride, and go find a pride for himself".

And when Ezekiel said "find", he meant the sex-orientated male lion would have to badly injure another lion and kill any young children that lion had recently fathered, in order to take his place. The rustling stopped, and we saw the mother in the little crop-circle they created, staring down her son, who mooched off.

I turned to my wife, whose face seemed a reflection of my thoughts. We were recently amused at the gazelle tradition. In their system the women hang out in one group, the men hang out in another group up to a mile away. The guys have a fight club, and whoever wins gets to join the girl gazelles where he indulges in an orgy of impregnation. He can stay as long as he is able to fend off the guy who comes over as winner of the next bachelor fight club. The challenge is that the guy in the harem is usually so knackered from all the sex, that he usually loses, and has to return to bachelor fight club and start again. This ensures the diversity of genes across the species and a never-dull atmosphere in both groups.

We had also reconciled ourselves – we thought – to other role differences between male lions and lionesses. The guys protect the pride; not against the non-lion enemy, because there isn't one. But against other male lions who want to do what they've already done: kill the head of pride and have sex with all the women. So they're protecting themselves, definitely, and their kids, maybe. But they're not really protecting the lionesses.

So other than that limited defence role, what do they do? Mainly, they go for long walks while the Mums play with and get hassled by the kids. Sometimes the guys hunt, sometimes the Mums hunt. When the guys hunt, they eat first. If they find nothing and have just been wandering around the savannah for a while, they start howling for the women at sunset to bring them some food. Meantime the Mums have been looking after the kids all day, except for when they do some hunting themselves. And even when the Dad is close to the rest of his family, he'll go find some long grass in which to chill out, just about in earshot of his progeny.

So we knew all of that, and for the most part we shrugged. But this: son tries to have sex with Mum when Dad's away, Mum beats son; son tries it again when Dad's around, Dad beats the crap out of son; son leaves home. That was a bit much.

I cast a disapproving glance at the frustrated teenage lion, and a sympathetic wince at his Mum as we drove off.

SOUKS

"One of the last pictures of the souk, maybe", said Youssef as I fiddled with the settings on my Nikon, hoping to find the button that says, 'Make it all look exactly as I see it'.

"Well, of course, yes; we have to go soon, right?"

He didn't hear me.

"All of this will be changed soon. All of it gone."

Wait, what? Our guide had projected a dignified and absurdly well-informed enthusiasm for the first four hours of our walking tour, but now he seemed wistful.

"Changing what?" I asked.

Youssef waved at this latest entrance of many, to the souk area of Medina: the old-town section of Marrakech, Morocco that held our attention more than any slow stroll round a congested city-centre had a right to.

"They're going to renovate it."

If my camera could talk it would have said, "Yes, PLEASE. FINALLY". The poor thing coped with an absurd array of lighting challenges since we set out mid-morning and the processor was having a hard day.

"Is that a bad thing?"

"You remember the building that looked like it was brand new?"

I did. It was ugly, almost colourless, and devoid of design. A functional blot on a dazzling, artistic cityscape.

"The entire souk area will be like that. And they're going to put a normal roof over all of it."

My eyes widened in shock.

"Like a mall," he continued.

My camera tried to voice its approval again, and I switched it off.

The mere use of the word 'mall' was mildly horrifying. The stores of the souk were full of filigreed lanterns with thousands of shafts of sunlight hitting them from numerous, changing angles all day, creating infinite changing patterns. The thought it might be razed made me feel ill. We had only been in Marrakech for a day, and I'm wary of falling in love with a place purely because it's different. But we already loved the place and the infinite playing of sunlight was one of the reasons.

"But why would they do that?"

"Because the king wants it."

"Why would the king want that? It's horrible!" I asked, in a much lower voice.

"He probably doesn't want it, but that's what people say he wants, so now you can't say anything."

It seems that the way to shut down a conversation in Morocco is to declare which side of the debate you believe King Mohamed VI is on, or simply which side you'd prefer him to be on, as if he already agreed with you. Once that is settled, the argument is settled. Yousef went on to explain about his conversations with a government architect, who couldn't understand Yousef's objections to the official plans.

"They don't visit the souk," Yousef said. "They don't know."

The souks (markets) are set in an impenetrable maze of roads in the middle of Medina, itself an area of Marrakech home to two of the three million city inhabitants. More or less. No-one's entirely sure what the percentages are, particularly as so many people from the poorer centre try to get their kids into the schools in modern (outer) Marrakech, which skews census numbers.

The entire area is pedestrianised; not because cars are not allowed but because they don't fit. Every road is between five and ten feet wide, with no sidewalks, providing almost day-long shade to the hordes of people making their way around. Overhead, most walls are connected to the those on the other side of the street by makeshift roofing to create shade for lunchtime ,when the sun arrows down between the buildings. The shades are made from long, thin branches laid on rope between the buildings, designed not to block the sunlight but merely disrupt it. They need the light, but not all the heat, so the branches, laid down parallel to each other, are not pushed together. The spaces between them don't merely illuminate, they create a festival of ever-moving light shafts hitting people, goods, storefronts and animals. Every few minutes during the middle part of the day, the scene changes as the light strikes some things square on and ricochets off others. And the unceasing throng from mid-morning onwards provides the canvas, the angles and the participants for the living art.

With everything and everyone so close, the sounds and smells are as intense as the light. You're never far from someone selling spices from open sacks, so the air is full of cumin, cinnamon, and cardamom. Every few minutes a donkey with a cart edges past, carrying its own factory of smells. Bread is for sale everywhere, from the specifically Moroccan batbout to the generic circular loaves dispensed from enormous piles in carts in each mini-square, and from neat stacks in tiny shop-window cabinets. Sheep hoof stew bubbles away on unattended stoves, and in the afternoons when the leather market is open for business, you can't help but want to buy shoes.

And yet the strongest smell is the exhaust from two-stroke engines. Slow, and yet dangerously quick mopeds and scooters, revving and dodging their way around the markets are the one thing I wished the central planners would get centrally planningy about. Because everything is so close, the sound is amplified and the smoke lingers, obliterating the olfactory spa that provides so much of the souk's appeal. Not that anyone seemed to mind the mopeds; so, after a time, neither did we. Two-stroke simply took its place next to cumin.

By lunchtime we were in one of the larger squares, and Yousef pointed at a series of second-storey rooftops overlooking the square, to which we might head for lunch.

"They're the ones recommended in all the guidebooks", he said. "We could eat at one of those" – he paused – "or we could eat local."

I was taken aback at the distinction, partly because I assumed that guidebooks wouldn't be recommending non-local restaurants in the centre of old town Marrakech. And to be fair, looking online at the menus of recommended (including Medina rooftop) restaurants in Marrakech, they all serve very local flavours. But they also have a tendency to dump fries in the middle of those local dishes, and to make great play of a view that – because every house is the same height – is more of a satellite dish conference than a city view.

As it turned out, the recommended rooftop restaurants also charge literally ten times as much as a more genuinely local, ground-level restaurants.

Yousef, visibly relieved at our choice of local over guidebook, ducked into an alley and within five strides had us outside an eatery you couldn't recommend in a guidebook because it didn't have a name, a phone number, or, seemingly, an address. Across the six-feet wide alleyway from its nearest competitor, the front of this eatery was a row of single-serving-sized tajines on wood fires in an open window.

'Tajine' is the word for both the dish and the clay cooking vessel. The latter is a clay dish, into which goes the food, and over which is placed a clay cone, resting on a ledge on the inside of the dish and with a hole at the top, like an upturned funnel with a very short pipe. Depending on where you are in the cooking process, the hole is either left open, or blocked with a carrot. The dish and funnel-cone sit snugly on an individual wood fire, made of clay. Inside the tajine, the tajine is cooked for several hours depending on the size of the dish. Typically it involves either a piece of two of lamb or chicken, surrounded by a tomato base, maybe some cous-cous, with large slabs of vegetable and potato resting on the sides of the meat.

The three of us ducked into the hole-in-the-wall restaurant and sat around the largest of the five tables. We ordered a tajine and mini loaf of still-warm flatbread each, with two Moroccan salads and a sardines-in-marinara offering to share. The potatoes were a marvel: soft on the inside with some crispiness on the outside, and after hours of cooking hadn't collapsed into mush. The ruddy spice mix infused everything, giving all the elements of the dish a uniform, deep and smoldering flavour.

As we readied to leave I glanced through the front door of the restaurant, ten feet from our table. Past the piles of warm bread and the row of tajines, light clouds of spicy smoke leaked into the alleyway and enveloped the comradely competition between vendors. We followed the clouds out, to lose ourselves again in seven hundred years of alleyways.

Later, after six hours wandering the souks with Yousef I put my exhausted Nikon back in its bag and walked away. The souks were noisy, polluted and claustrophobic. But to leave them was to feel burdened by silence, to crave their smells and yearn for their intensity.

As we made to leave, the relentlessly helpful Yousef turned, looked at the camera bag and then at me. "Are you done?" he asked.

I hope not.

A DISAGREEMENT

'Mister Dalton, you are representing yourself?'

'Yes, Your Worship. Ma'am.'

'"Your Worships' are magistrates, 'Ma'am' smacks of indolent rank, and I am neither. I must recommend that you do not represent yourself, Mister Dalton, although that is. Your. Choice.

And 'Your Honour' or 'Judge Dent' will do.'

Andy replied that yes, he intended to represent himself.

'It's gone ten to twelve, late start, I cannot to give you any extra time, and Mister Dalton you have applied to the court to counter.'

She paused. Andy and Suzanne leaned forward in their seats while Suzanne's lawyer stared at the ceiling.

The judge leaned forward to prompt: 'You wish to contest Missus Dalton's divorce application on the grounds of your wife's unreasonable behaviour which you say started from the outset of your relationship and persisted through your cohabitation and has-'

Judge Dent removed her glasses and placed them with their arms out on her desk. Then she put them back on her face and exhaled noisily - the only sound in the room.

'-carried on through your marriage to the present day.'

Was that a question or a statement? 'We just need to get lawyers involved to make sure we do it properly', Suzanne had told him months earlier, 'we don't want to make a mess of it'. This judge seemed to be making things more, rather than less, messy.

'Counter, your Ladyship?'

'Judge.'

'Sorry Judge.'

'Are you attempting to agree to the divorce but disagree on the grounds of the divorce, or are you disagreeing with the divorce per se, or are you disagreeing with the divorce because you want Missus Dalton to withdraw her divorce application so that you can apply for a divorce. Yourself?'

Authority was intimidating; expectant, complicated authority doubly so. Andy, needing time to decipher this question and remember the previous one, moved his gaze away from the judge's eyes, past her left ear and onto a blank wall interrupted by a window, with the venetian blind closed. He noticed a bent slat, testimony to the previous afternoon when the judge spent fifteen minutes peering out at a suspected car thief who she was relieved to see walk away from the car. Although when she returned to her car that evening, a window was broken and her iPad was missing.

Above the blind with the bent slat, a digital clock, reassuring him: 11.55am. He hadn't used a digital clock since he left his parents' house and moved in with Suzanne, eight years ago yesterday. Suzanne hated digital clocks. 'Digital clocks are like nobody can tell the time themselves so someone has to tell it to them. Analog all the way. It's either me or that,' she waved at his clock, 'child's thing,' she said at the time. She nodded with disdain at the digital clock he was about to put on his bedside table, but followed it with one of her tidal smiles and Andy smiled back, threw the clock in a box. Andy's moods were like the pebbles on the beach, pushed up when the tide came in; dragged down, he felt, when the tide of her smile went out.

'Mister Dalton,' a formal voice insisted to him from far away.

Three years and one day ago – their high water mark - they got married. Andy remembered being happy, despite the analog clock on the wall in the registry office. Suzanne was happy too, and hadn't noticed the clock. A year after that Suzanne became pregnant with 'Oops', who became Katie. Two years ago Andy lost his job with the insurance company; soon after that the tide went out permanently and they stopped having sex or talking of anything beyond logistics.

Suzanne was still pregnant with Oops when they started counselling. The counsellor was a woman, the clock was analog, and Suzanne talked to the counsellor of Andy's 'passivity'. Towards her, towards work, towards everything. He argued, of course, as much to prove his non-passivity as to make a substantive point, and demanded to change counsellors. He checked out a couple of alternatives, with particularly attention to what kind of timepiece they mounted on their walls, but they kept going for a few months to the one she liked.

Not like this digital clock today, with the red numbers, currently reading eleven fifty-six. With a tiny 'A.M.', for clarity. It was the precision, he realised, that comforted him, and yet his favourite clock was the one in the registry office. He'd give anything to be in front of that clock again.

'I'm disagreeing, Judge Your Honour.'

Thanks for reading.

I hope you enjoyed this collection of stories. We would appreciate your feedback, please consider leaving a review.